LEISURE
BOOKS

$5.99 US
$7.99 CAN
$14.95 AUS

W9-CYU-039

50599

0-8439-2484-5

9 780843 924848

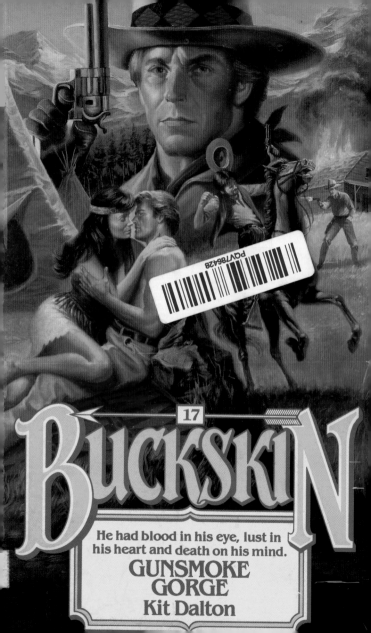

17

BUCKSKIN

He had blood in his eye, lust in
his heart and death on his mind.

GUNSMOKE
GORGE

Kit Dalton

A DEADLY BRAWL

Morgan stayed put. He caught a glimpse of a shadow just to his right. He turned and heard the doors open. Two shots rang out. Both from outside. *Culpepper.* Morgan thought so. He took advantage of the distraction and took a chance. He moved three feet to his right, removed his hat and tossed it onto the end of the bar just above where he'd been, and then he stood up.

Morgan's hat flew from the bar just as he shot Louie Blanchard, one of Jess Blanchard's brothers, right between the eyes.

Also in the *Buckskin* Series:

BUCKSKIN #17

GUNSMOKE GORGE

KIT DALTON

LEISURE BOOKS NEW YORK CITY

A LEISURE BOOK®

August 2004

Published by

Dorchester Publishing Co., Inc.
200 Madison Avenue
New York, NY 10016

ISBN 0-8439-2484-5

Printed in the United States of America.

Visit us on the web at www.dorchesterpub.com.

1

The main street of Grover, Idaho, was decked out in banners, ribbons, flags and wreaths. They were all *black!* Many of the store fronts were boarded up and Lee Morgan saw no sign of life. He was still looking up and down the street when he finally dismounted in front of the Sawtooth saloon. Clearly, the little cowtown was in mourning . . . but for *who?* Almost everyone of any prominence had long since died or moved on.

The Sawtooth was empty, save for the barkeep. He was a nervous little man, somewhat porcine in appearance. When Morgan entered, he looked up, over top of the pince-nez glasses he was wearing. He started to smile but then he spotted Morgan's gun. His expression changed to fear and his hands shook as he put down the beer mug he was wiping.

"Y . . . yessir?"

"A beer," Morgan said. It wasn't what he wanted but it was quick and easy. He was too curious about conditions to spend much time here now. He watched the barkeep draw the draught with shaking hands.

"Fifteen cents," the man said.

"Keeps gettin' higher, doesn't it?"

"The distributor out of Boise just raised the price again last week."

5

Morgan nodded, took a long swallow and then said, "Who died?"

"Beg pardon?"

"Who died?" Morgan repeated. At the same time, he gestured toward the street. "Must have been somebody pretty damned important."

"Then . . . you, uh, you're not from around here?"

"Not lately."

"Lots o' folks," the barkeep said. Morgan considered him. He went on. "They're buryin' eight 's'afternoon."

"Eight?"

"The Winslows. Joad an' his missus. Frank Peters who worked for him an' a cowhand name o' Kane." Morgan pondered the name but it didn't register.

"That's only four," he finally said.

"The others I never knowed a 'tall. Folks had a ranch close by, mebbe three, four mile."

"What ranch? The name I mean."

"Don't recollect right off." The little barkeep frowned and then shook his head and waggled a finger in the air. "Somethin' odd." Morgan straightened up. "Differ'nt," the barkeep added. Suddenly he smiled. "That's right . . . cards. Name had to do with cards. It was the Spade Bit Ranch."

Morgan never finished the beer. He rode the big bay hard all the way . . . all four miles. There was a chill wind sweeping down from the north when Morgan finally reined up. He pulled up his coat collar and jammed his hat down tighter. He was on a rise along the Jack's Fork tributary of the Wickahoney River. He looked at the valley below.

"Jeezus!" Morgan felt the hair at the back of his neck bristle. His cheeks flushed with anger. The once lush valley was charred and only a lone brick chimney still stood. It seemed a mute sentry guarding burned memories against the advent of an unseen threat. The Spade Bit Ranch was gone!

Morgan rode down, slowly. He remembered. The big, white frame house. The old barn and smoke house. The bunk houses and the cook shack. Indians? Morgan doubted that. It was 1877 when the last of the Red Men posed any threat in Idaho. The Nez Perce, a small band trying to escape to Canada. General Oliver O. Howard finally cornered them and their leader, a Chief named Joseph.

Maybe they'd jumped the reservation. Morgan thought back to what he'd heard. Joseph had finally surrendered in the winter snows. The army had lied to him again—even in his defeat. He was separated from the rest of his people, sent to a far away reservation in Washington or Oregon. Then Morgan remembered the old Chief's promise. Morgan repeated the words aloud. "From where the sun now stands, I will fight no more . . . forever!" Morgan looked around again. He felt anger. "The hell I won't fight," he said.

He rode on another mile. The undulations of the land built to another rise, a sharp rise. Atop a quiet hill, beneath a huge, century old Willow, there was a small cemetery. Morgan dismounted and walked to its crest. He sought out a single headstone and stood, quietly, hat in hand, looking at the name engraved upon it.

William Frank Leslie

"I know what you'd do daddy," Morgan finally said. "I guess you got the only peace there is."

Morgan found the nervous little barkeep in the

Sawtooth was no longer alone. He was talking to a big, round shouldered man. Both of them looked up when Morgan entered.

"That's *him*," the barkeep whispered. He stepped behind the bar and the big man stepped away from it.

"Hold it mister." As he spoke, the man produced an old model Navy Colt's. He levelled it at Morgan's belly. "I'm Marshal Rawlings."

"Seth?" Morgan stepped to the bar where the light was better. "Seth . . . it's Lee. Lee Morgan."

"Lee Morgan?" The marshal moved closer, but he didn't lower the gun. "I'll be," he finally said. Morgan started to move toward him, his hand extended in friendship. The marshal backed off. "Who you ridin' with?"

"What?" Morgan stopped. "Seth, maybe you didn't hear me."

"I heard you. Question's still the same. Who you ridin' with?"

"Nobody. What the hell is going on here? I just rode back from the Spade Bit or what's left of it. Jeezus, Seth, I'd like some answers."

"So would I," the marshal said, "an' mebbe I can get some of 'em from you. Ease the gun onto the bar —real slow like." The marshal cocked the old Colt's and Morgan knew he wasn't kidding. Morgan complied and the marshal motioned for Morgan to walk to the door. "Over to my office. You remember where?"

"I remember."

"What if he's got riders with 'im," the barkeep said, softly. Morgan heard the question. "I don't. I haven't seen anybody in Grover since I rode in except you two."

"You start walkin'," the marshal said. "Stay well

ahead o' me but you'd best not try anythin'. No runnin' . . . no signallin'. You try it Morgan an' I may die but you'll go first.''

"Let's go," Morgan said. "Let's get over to your office and get this cleared up."

Morgan found himself an old high-backed, wooden chair and sat down on it, backwards. Seth Rawlings layed the Bisley on his desk, holstered his own gun and then sat on the desk's edge.

"How long you been back, boy?"

"I got here today."

"From where?"

"Cheyenne. Look, Seth . . ."

"I'll do the askin' boy, you do the answerin' . . . fer now anyways." Morgan shrugged. "Somebody send fer ya?"

"No."

"You hear 'bout anythin' goin' on up this way before you rode back?"

"No." Morgan was getting irritated. Seth could detect it. He shifted his position for easier access to his gun. "I came back to see some old friends, maybe go to ranching."

"You mean cow herdin'?"

"I *mean* ranching. I was planning to look for a spread."

"You picked a poor time," Seth said. "Poor time fer ranchin', poor time for findin' work, poor time to come back." The old lawman got up, walked behind his desk and began thumbing through a stack of wanted posters.

"You won't find anything on me Seth." The marshal ignored him and finished going through the stack.

"I got nothin' here an' nothin' to hold you on." He handed Morgan the Bisley. "Where you headed now that you know about the Spade Bit?"

"I don't know Seth. Not right this minute anyway."

"Lemme help you boy. Sarah Brownin' is runnin' a boardin' house now. As I recollect, you 'n Sarah thought a little more'n most 'bout each other. Not much business lately, she could prob'ly use your money."

Morgan frowned. "Sarah was . . ."

"Married? Yeah, fer a spell. He was a tin horn. Rode over to Boise one day 'bout two, mebbe three years back. Never come home ag'in."

"Well, then, maybe I will stay with her."

"You do that, Lee. Git yourself a good night's sleep an' then why don't you ride on out? Back south mebbe, back to Cheyenne."

"Damn it, Seth," Morgan said, standing now, "you're right. You got nothing on me in that stack of posters and nothing to hold me on . . . so why you pushing me?"

"I'm not pushin' you boy . . . I'm givin' you some sound advice. Take it. It's free."

"And so am I Seth. Free as a goddamn bird. When you were sheriff you pushed hard. Well, I was a hot-tempered, short fused kid then, I'm not anymore."

"An' I'm not sheriff. I'm a United States Terri-torial Marshal and I don't need any hired guns ridin' in."

"Seems to be Seth, from the look of the Spade Bit, you got plenty of 'em. Maybe you ought to get some of them on your side."

Seth Rawlings walked to the door, opened it and then turned back. "Sarah's place is a block south."

Sarah Browning, like 'most everyone else, was at the furnerals. One of her guests, a whiskey drummer, told Morgan she wouldn't be back until late. There was to be a big community feed at the church after the services.

Morgan thanked the drummer and left. He considered going to the church but finally decided against it. There were many, he was sure, who probably wouldn't take kindly to the son of a gunman, himself possessed of a dubious reputation, showing up. Besides, Morgan still had plenty of questions and no answers. He rode northeast out of town. He knew one place he might get them.

2

It was a long, rugged trip from Grover up to the Rocky Barr ranch. Morgan rode onto R-B land a full day before the house would come into sight. It was northeast from Grover, up toward the Sawtooth range.

He forded the south fork of the Boise River and was following one of the R-B's fence lines when he found himself confronted with two surly looking young men.

"What the fuck you doin' here mister?"

"My name is . . . ."

"I didn't *ask* your fuckin' name. I ask what you're doin' up here?"

Morgan eyed both men. They were gunnys . . . no doubt about that. Morgan could remember the days when Judge Isaac Barr would have run such men as these off his property . . . or had them hanged!

"You take me to the *Judge*," Morgan said. "I'll talk to him."

"You'll talk to me or you won't live long enough to see the goddam *Judge*."

The man reached behind him. Morgan could see the stock of the rifle. He looked at the other man who was smiling and fingering the butt of his pistol. Morgan shrugged. He swung his right leg over the pommel and dropped to the ground. The move covered his release of the Black Snake whip from its leather retainer.

The man with the rifle brought the weapon to bear. Morgan's right arm went back in a smooth, flowing arc. The whip lashed out.

"Jeezus!" A long, red gash suddenly appeared on the back of the man's hand. The rifle slipped from his grip and clattered to the ground. Morgan dropped to his left knee, hauled back his right arm, rolled to his left and thus avoided being shot. The whip was ready again and caught the second man, who'd fired at Morgan, across the right cheek. He grabbed at his face, losing his pistol in the act.

Now, there was a double sound. The whip's narrow mass slicing the air and the crack of its tip against flesh . . . horse flesh! First one . . . then the other . . . both whinnied and bolted off, full bore.

Judge Isaac Holston Barr was pushing sixty. Few men knew it for he looked closer to forty-five. He had once boasted that he'd have no man working for him that he couldn't whip. By his look, the rule might still apply.

He was a short man, barely five and a half feet. He was barrel chested, bull-necked and with arms that resembled logs. His torso was nearly as long as his legs, which were bowed from years in the saddle. He walked straight, fast and rarely looked up to any man.

Rumor had it that he'd once been a pugilist back east. He admitted only that he had entered the prize ring to earn extra money while he attended law school. The *Judge* sobriquet was not honorary but a fact. He'd served the circuit for a dozen years.

"I'll be damned," Judge Barr said. Lee Morgan stepped from his mount and secured the reins to the hitching rail.

"Judge."

"I was about to send out half a dozen men to string up the bastard who'd use a black snake on a man."

"It still ain't right," the tall man standing next to the Judge said.

"Beats dyin' Harper." Judge Barr turned to the tall man. "That's what would have happened if this young fella had used his gun instead of the whip. You might want to remember that."

Morgan stopped on the first step. He held out his hand. Judge Barr took it, shook it warmly and put his other hand on Morgan's shoulder.

"If I'd have been anywhere but on Rocky Barr land, those two gunnys would be laying out there right now. It's good to see you, Judge," Morgan said.

"I'm glad you didn't kill them. I need every man I've got." He turned, stepped onto the porch and motioned with his head for Morgan to follow. "C'mon in." The man called Harper stepped between the judge and Morgan just as Lee started to move. Their eyes met. Harper fingered the butt of his pistol. Morgan smiled, sidestepped quickly and walked on by him.

"What'll you be drinkin'?"

"Bourbon's fine," Morgan replied.

"Sit, son," Judge Barr said. He handed Morgan a glass. "Tell me about yourself." Morgan did. "What brought you back to the Idaho?"

"An idea," Morgan replied, blandly. "A bad idea."

"The Spade Bit?"

"Yeah. What the hell's going on Judge?"

"East of the Mississippi they call it progress."

"What do *you* call it?"

"Thievery!"

"Who's doin' it . . . and why?"

"The last part's easy," the judge said. "Land. They've got more beef on the hoof than they can graze. Ten . . . fifteen years back they started leasing land. The locals jumped at it . . . didn't think to the future. Lease money meant a steady income during tough winters and three meals a day for the sodbusters whose crops didn't make it."

"And now?"

"The leases are up and the ranchers are getting their notes called in."

"Notes?"

"The lease agreements all had riders . . . options on them. They allowed the small operations to borrow extra money against the lease contracts. Many of them took advantage of it and got in way over their heads. Borrowed more than the lease money would ever pay back."

"They're foreclosing."

"Uh huh. And anybody who stands against them gets run out, burned out or killed."

"I take it from what you say that it's not gettin' settled in the courts."

"Nothing to settle. The leases were legal, the money borrowed on them is due and payable. Thing is, most of the smaller farmers and ranchers signed direct . . . no legal advice. There was a renewal option in every lease but the fine print was another matter."

"How so?"

"*If* the owner wanted to excercise his renewal option, he had ninety days to do it and signed over half his spread if he did."

"Jeezus!"

"Like I said . . . thievery. Me, the folks down on your old place, Josh Killerman over on the Snake River ranch and a few other outfits didn't sign. Most of us didn't need the help but we also knew what they had planned. We tried to warn the smaller ranchers. Even formed an association. They just saw us as harbingers of doom."

"And now?"

"Most of them are already out. Thing is, it's starting to hurt the bigger outfits like me. I'm hemmed in now on three sides. If two or three of the smaller outfits south of here buckle I'll have no way to move stock."

"They'll own the land and won't let you cross it." The Judge smiled, cynically. "They'll let me cross it . . . sure . . . for a *fee!*"

"And there's not a damned thing you can do about it?"

"Just one. We've already been through the courts. We lost but it did buy us some time. We organized a few of the smaller outfits and pulled them into the Rancher's Association. Me, Killerman, Ben Strada . . . some of the wealthier outfits put up money to tide the little fellows over the rough spots."

"Holdouts."

"Yes . . . and the outfit back east . . . and we don't know for sure just who it is . . . can't wait. They've got *really* big money in this. Railroad money and buyers who are waiting."

"You hoped to bust their backs that way," Morgan said. "Figuring they'd back off?"

"Yes . . . but they got rough instead. Our only chance is catching the sons-o'-bitches red handed. We do that, we might have a tie to somebody back east."

"Doesn't sound like you've had much luck so far."

"Plenty of luck Morgan . . . all bad. I've got a few gunnys working for me . . . mostly trying to protect my own place. So do some of the others, but we've got no one who can stand against these marauders. They hit and run. They're good. Nobody wants to go up against them."

"Well," Morgan said, getting to his feet, "the marshal told me it was a hell of a bad time to come home. I guess he was right."

The judge frowned. "You walking away from it?"

"It's not my fight, Judge. I didn't come back to fight and there's nothing left to buy . . . at least for me."

"That's not the kind of thing your daddy would have said."

"I'm *not* Frank Leslie, Judge. Oh I thought about it. When I saw the Bit . . . walked up to my dad's hole in the ground . . . I thought about it. I was mad. I also thought it was just somebody had something against the Bit. Sorry, Judge. This is not for me."

"Morgan . . . do me one favor."

"If I can, Judge . . . I will."

"I've hired one man . . . one *damned good* man. He'll be here in a few days, three at the most. Stay with me . . . wait 'til he gets here and then sit in a meeting with us. That's all I'm asking."

"Who's the man?"

"I'd sooner not say 'til you see him. How about it?"

"I owe you. Sounds like that might square us. No promises beyond that."

"Agreed."

"I'll pass staying, Judge. Thanks anyway but I've got an itch to ride to Boise. I'll be back. You've got my word."

"Good enough, Morgan."

* * *

Boise was probably Idaho's answer to Wichita,
Dodge City or any of the plains country cow towns.
The westward trek of humanity in the sixties and
seventies had, finally, brought some law and order
to those towns. By the mid to late eighties, men like
Morgan's father, the Masterson types, the Earps,
had weeded out most of the killers. North of the
major trails however, towns like Boise were ten to
fifteen years behind the times.

Morgan was amazed at how much Boise had
grown but it still looked like a prairie twister had
simply dsposited it where it sat. There was little
rhyme nor reason to its layout and there were three
blocks devoted solely to a man's basic needs. One
gunsmith, twelve saloons and fifteen brothels.
Morgan reined up in front of the most lavish of the
pleasure palaces, The Four Queens.

It boasted a fine saloon, private baths, a client's
personal tonsorial services and the best ladies
money could buy. Morgan moved to the bar.

"You wantin' any upstairs service," the barkeep
asked him.

"No."

"Then the prices for drinks are posted on the wall
behind me. What'll you have?"

"Is Belle in?" The question brought raised
eyebrows from the barkeep and the shuffling of feet
off to Morgan's left. He glanced in the backbar's
mirror and caught sight of a tall, well dressed,
menacing type. He was standing in front of a door
which said *Office* on it.

"Who wants to know?"

"Lee Morgan." The barkeep's eyes shifted over
Morgan's left shoulder. Morgan glanced into the
mirror again and the tall man was walking toward

the bar. Morgan did a half turn.

"I don't recall Miss Moran mentioning any appointments this morning."

"I don't have an appointment, but if you'll tell her the name, I will have."

"You seem damned sure of that, Mister Morgan."

"Why don't you try it?"

"After you tell me the reason I'll consider it."

"The reason is my business," Morgan said, "all you have to do is tote a message."

"I don't like you, Mister Morgan."

"Then by all means, let's keep our business as brief as possible."

The man's left hand slipped from the bar and moved toward his left hip. The barkeep had just bent forward, his hands disappearing beneath the bar. Morgan made one step backwards and both men found themselves staring at the business end of his Bisley Colt's. "Don't even *think* about it," Morgan said. "I want to see two sets of hands up on that bar . . . palms down . . . right *now*!" He punctuated the request with the click of the Bisley's hammer. The men complied.

"I repeat," Morgan said, "is Belle in?" The tall man nodded. "Office?" He nodded again. Morgan smiled. "Now tell the son-of-a-bitch up on the balcony to put down the scatter-gun and back off. Then you walk right straight to that office ahead of me and remember, you'll be the first to go."

"Back off Charlie . . . it's . . . it's okay. Put the shotgun down." The man complied. The tall man glanced at the barkeep and then turned and walked toward the office. Morgan fell in behind him.

He knocked. "Miss Moran . . . a gent to see you. Says his name is Lee Morgan."

A muffled voice responded. "Lee Morgan! Kee-

rist!'' The door flew open. The tall man stepped
aside. Belle Moran eyed the Colt's. Morgan holstered it. She gave the tall man a look of disgust and
then threw both arms around Morgan's neck.

Belle Morgan was, in fact, Mary Elizabeth
Cochran Moran, late of Seattle, Washington. She
was a year or two on the wrong side of thirty-five
and called herself, facetiously, a grass widow. Her
late husband was reposing beneath it, victim of a
fifth ace in a winning poker pot. She bedded the
man who shot him, dragged him back to Boise and
they jointly opened the brothel with two other
ladies. He christened it the *King & 3 Queens*. His
unwanted advances, a year later, against a fourth
girl resulted in his demise—and a new name. Belle
simply figured the new girl had done what she would
have eventually had to do anyway.

Belle had added an inch or two here and there, but
Morgan supposed she could make as good a use of
those as she did the rest. She had firm, large breasts
of which plenty was always visible. Her face was
full, round and displayed a perpetual smile. Her lips,
generously painted, were wide and sensuous and
Morgan knew what she could do with them.

"You've grown," she said, eyeing him. Her eyes
found his crotch. "Everywhere?"

"Why don't *you* be the judge of that," he said.

"Yeah Lee . . . why don't I?" She moved over and
locked the door. Morgan had already removed his
rig, shirt and belt. Belle Moran did the rest. Morgan
poured himself a drink, slipped onto the bed and
rested against its headboard. Belle stripped . . .
slowly.

He got hard just watching her. How long had it
been? He thought back. God! Cheyenne . . . five
weeks ago.

Belle didn't bed anyone unless *she* made the choice. When she did there was nothing better. Morgan, of course, had long since concluded that there was no such thing as a bad screw, only good, better, best and by God, fantastic! Belle Moran was at the head of the class.

She worked her tongue along the inside of his legs, alternating every few inches. Where they came together, she excelled. She traced invisible paths around, along and beneath his shaft. At the same time, the light touch of her fingers caressed below it and paused at the most sensitive junctures.

Morgan's eyes closed and the empty glass slipped from his hands. He moaned softly as she increased the speed and intensity of her ministrations. "It's been a hell of a while," he said. It was a warning that he might react too soon. Belle knew what to do. She climbed onto the bed, straddled Morgan about waist level and leaned forward. She moved from side to side, her breasts brushing his cheeks, the nipples bouncing off his nose or darting across his lips before he could catch one of them.

He finally reached up, his hands closed around them and his fingers pressed on their swollen tips. Belle stiffened, her head went back and goose bumps popped up and ran the length of her body like a sudden rash. As he continued caressing, she eased forward until her own, damp womanhood rested over his face. He licked. She groaned and then steeled herself for what was to come.

Wave after wave of delight surged through her body. Suddenly, she reversed herself and the two of them shared oral delight. At the very peak of pleasure, she reversed herself again, slipped his shaft inside herself and they fell to a steady but mounting rhythm.

"God . . . yes . . . yes Lee," she said. "Oh . . . faster
. . . do it faster." Together, they ascended passion's
peak and the summit was conquered in a wild,
sweaty, moaning instant. Lee Morgan's body
arched upwards and Belle Moran's lifted for just a
moment. They hung, suspended in pleasure, came
together for a final, crushing embrace and collapsed
in delighted exhaustion.

Morgan poured himself a drink and opted to try
one of Belle's store bought, pre-rolled smokes. That
done, he began to dress. Belle finally stirred and sat
up.

"Would you pour me a drink, honey?" Morgan
did. He handed it to her. She smiled. "You're better
than ever . . . but what brought you back?"

"The thought of staying put . . . maybe having
something besides a horse, a rifle and a reputation."

"I heard about the Bit."

"Yeah," Morgan said, scathingly, "so much for
staying put."

"It isn't the only spread in Idaho."

"It was the only one I might have dealt on . . . besides, there's trouble here . . . big trouble from the
way Judge Barr tells it."

Morgan turned and looked straight at Belle. "You
know anything about it?"

She downed the last of her drink, slipped from the
bed and put on a dressing gown. "Just enough to
want to stay out."

"Yeah Belle . . . me too."

"You driftin' again then?"

"Prob'ly. I promised the judge I'd stop back at
his place in a couple of days . . . after that, well, I
don't know."

"You can come to work for me," she said. She
moved close to him and even after what they had

just done, he could feel a stirring in his groin. "How about it?"

"I don't do well working for somebody Belle . . . never have."

"It wouldn't be the same here . . . you *know* that Lee."

"I'll think on it," he said. "My poke tells me I'll have to do *something* . . . and pretty damned quick."

"You need a touch Lee . . . you know where to come."

A ruckus in the street got both their attentions. Belle stepped to the window and pulled back the curtain. Morgan saw a hulk of a man with a woman in his arms. Tears streamed down his face and two kids, a boy and a girl, trailed behind him. Both were crying.

"That's Ole' Thomassen," Belle said.

"Customer of yours."

"Not Ole'. God! That's his wife. He's takin' her into the Doc's office." She let the curtain drop and began to dress. She caught Morgan's quizzical expression. "Ole' had a bad crop two years back. I put him out front . . . bouncin' for me."

"A married man? With a family?"

"One o' my girls got carried off one time, beat up bad. The men dumped her about a half a mile from Ole's place. They took her in. His missus saved her life."

Morgan strapped on the Colt's and followed Belle through the Four Queens and across the street. Inside Doc Loudon's office, big Ole' sat in a chair, his face buried in his hands. His kids sat at his feet. They were all crying. Morgan walked into the doc's back room.

"Get out," the doc said, without looking up. "I don't need an audience. This will be difficult enough

as it is." Morgan didn't push it. Back outside, Belle
was just straightening up. She'd been talking to
Ole' and trying to comfort the children. She looked
solemn.

"The marauders hit his place, just before sunup.
He was on his way to town. The kids hid in the
storm cellar. His wife didn't make it."

"Burn him out?" She nodded. "He know who?"

"He didn't say, but I got a hunch he knows more
than he's lettin' out."

The front door opened and Belle and Morgan
looked up into the face of Tate Bosley, Boise's
sheriff. Belle filled him in but she was cut
short when Doc Loudon stepped out of his back
room. Everyone looked up. His teeth were clenched,
his hands still bloody. He shook his head. Ole'
Thomassen leaned back in the chair and let out a
pain-filled cry.

3

Morgan walked into Tate Bosley's office and found the sheriff filling out papers. Bosley looked up.

"Belle arranged for the Thomassen kids to have bed and board over at Miller's Boarding House. Ole' highttailed out of town. Nobody's sure where. Three or four gunnys have ridden in since morning and you're doing paper work. Why?"

Bosley wasn't ruffled. " 'Cause that's my job son . . . part of it anyways."

"What the hell happened to getting a posse up?" Bosley finished what he was doing and signed it. He slipped the sheet into a metal basket which held a dozen or more similar reports and then he got to his feet.

"You're Lee Morgan aren't you?" Morgan nodded. "You want to be deputized?"

"No."

"Well neither did fifteen or twenty others I asked . . . so, no posse. That paper I was working on is a report of what happened. I'll mail that off to the territorial marshal and ask for help. Should have an answer in a week . . . ten days maybe. Might even get the army stirred up if this keeps happenin'."

"Jesus Christ, Sheriff . . . what the hell are you saying? Shit! Men like my daddy would have had those bastards run down and strung up by now."

"Prob'ly Morgan. Old Frank Leslie was quite a fella." Now, Bosley's tone hardened along with his demeanor. "But this ain't eighteen and seventy five an' I'm no goddam Buckskin Frank or Bill Hickok." He pointed a gnarled finger at Morgan. "An' neither are you boy . . . so don't try to be. We got law. I grant you it ain't caught up with the country we're in yet, but if you don't start somewhere, you end up with no law at all."

"And none of these spineless bastards will ride posse?"

Bosley grinned. "They're not gunmen. They're storekeepers. Hell, half of 'em don't know one end of a Winchester from another. If you came in here lookin' for fast answers, son, you've wasted your time. I would have put a posse out . . . if I could have got one . . . but it wouldn't have done any good. Since I couldn't the only thing left is the paperwork."

"What do you carry that goddamn thing for?" Morgan asked, pointing to Bosley's hip.

"Because it's still legal."

"But you've never *used* it?"

Bosley grinned. "*This* end," he said, touching the butt. "Prob'ly put eight or ten notches on it. Drunks, a tinhorn or two. Puts 'em to sleep. Then I can usually get one o' the upstandin' citizens of Boise to help me tote 'em over here so's they can sleep it off."

Morgan's face flushed. He turned on his heels and jerked the door open.

"Morgan." Lee turned. "Don't use the Bisley . . . less'n somebody tries to kill you . . . and you'd best have a witness or two. Use it any other way . . . I'll come after you . . . unless you want *this.*" He held out a badge. Morgan slammed the door.

Morgan had no more than walked through the

front door of the Four Queens when he was confronted by Belle.

"Ole' Thomassen just left here." Morgan looked past Belle and saw the tall, menacing looking man in a heap on the floor. "I think he busted Steve's jaw. He wanted a shotgun. He's headed for the Boise Hotel."

"Did he get the shotgun?" She nodded. Morgan wheeled and hurried to his horse. The Boise was two blocks away. He didn't tether his mount, he just let the reins drop. He could hear screams from inside the hotel's lobby and he moved quickly to where he could see in the window.

Ole' Thomassen had scattered about everybody. Eight or nine people, mostly well dressed, were kneeling, crouching or otherwise trying to stay out of the way. Ole' was looking up. So did Morgan.

Two men stood at the head of the stairway. Both wore store bought suits. Morgan could see the telltale bulges of shoulder holsters. He also caught sight of a third man . . . far to Ole's right. He also had a shotgun.

Morgan opened the door, carefully and stepped just inside.

"Ay know who done it . . . ay know he's up there. Ay, by golly, will kill him."

"Go home old man . . . you've come sniffing around the wrong tree."

"Ay'm comin' up . . . an' nobody, by golly, better get in Ole's way."

Ole' started up the stairway. Eight steps went to a landing and then it turned right and went up six more to the balcony. Morgan watched the two men at the top of the stairs. When Ole' Thomassen reached the landing, one of them nodded. Morgan stepped out of the foyer, whirled to his right, drew and fired.

"Shoot, Ole'," he yelled. Morgan's shot killed the
man with the shotgun instantly. Reflexes fired his
weapon and it tore a bucket sized hole in the ceiling.
Morgan turned back in time to see a wide-eyed Ole'
Thomassen take two .38 slugs high in his chest.
Morgan took out the man nearest his own position
and the man's body tumbled toward Ole'. The action
prevented the second man from firing. Morgan was
shocked by what happened next.

Ole' dropped his shotgun, grabbed his chest and
staggered back a step. Then, shaking his head as
though he was recovering from a surprise fist to his
jaw, he lowered his head and charged up the remaining steps. The second man in the fancy suit lost his
weapon. Ole' had him around the waist.

"Ole' . . . let him go, drop him, Ole'," Morgan
shouted. "This is no good." His words were futile.
Ole' tightened his grip. He was lifting the man from
the floor, slamming him down again and with each
movement, increasing his bear hug. Soon, only Ole's
labored breathing could be heard. The man let go a
moan or two and tried to put his hands up to Ole's
face and neck to free himself. A moment later, there
was a series of barely audible, snapping sounds.
Ribs gave way. Lungs were punctured. The man
coughed blood. His head drooped to one side. Ole'
Thomassen turned him loose.

Ole's own exertion had merely shortened the time
he had left. Even his brute strength was no match
for two .38 caliber bullets. The door opened behind
Morgan. Tate Bosley burst through it. He saw
Morgan and looked up. Ole' staggered, tried to
regain his balance and then crashed through the
bannister and fell thirty feet to the marble floor. It
broke his neck.

Even as the scene unfolded, two men had slipped from the room at the end of the hall, hurried down an iron fire escape and were already riding, hard, out of town.

"I'll have your gun, Morgan." Lee was crouched over Ole's body.

"He broke his neck. He's dead."

"I said . . . I'll have your gun." Morgan's hand was like lightening. He slipped Bosley's own pistol from the holter, let it slide into his palm until he could grip the barrel and brought the butt down on Bosley's skull. The sheriff collapsed. Morgan rolled him over, replaced the pistol and hurried outside. A few minutes later, he was riding the trail back to the northeast . . . back toward the Rocky Barr Ranch.

"That's a rotten damned shame," Judge Barr said, after hearing Morgan's story. "Ole' Thomassen worked for me once . . . eight, mebbe nine years back. Worked like an ox. Saved every penny." The judge shook his head. "An' two fine youngsters orphaned." He turned and looked Lee Morgan straight in the eye. "You see what we're up against. Can you ride away from *that*?"

"You told me you had hired a man . . . *one* man. Who the hell is he, Judge, Hickok's ghost?"

"He rode in late last night. You'll meet him at dinner. He's already got a plan. Right now, there's someone else I want you to meet . . . just back from a trip to San Francisco."

In the Rocky Barr's parlor, Lee Morgan found himself face-to-face with one of the most strikingly beautiful women he'd ever seen. She was very fair and her hair, a golden blonde, was swept up at her neck and piled in orderly curls upon her head. Her features appeared almost sculptured, slim nose, small but perfectly formed lips and closely set, hazel eyes.

Her throat was creamy white, long and tapered into a chest which supported two, perfectly rounded, firm breasts. The turquoise gown exposed much of both of them. Her waist was wasp-like and hips flared into long legs which Morgan could only suppose were as perfect as the rest he could see.

"This is Lee Morgan," Judge Barr said. He moved over and put his arm around the woman's waist and moved her toward Morgan. She held out her hand. "You two have something . . . almost in common." Morgan looked quizzical.

"Our names," she said, smiling. "Mine's Morgana . . . Morgana Barr."

"She's my daughter."

"My pleasure," Morgan said. He struggled to keep his eyes from drifting downward again. She smiled and held his hand for what seemed a somewhat inappropriate length of time.

The dining room was crowded. Over a dozen, well dressed men milled about chattering. Most looked stern. Morgan, hardly dressed for the occasion, found himself a somewhat out of the way corner. He sipped bourbon. Judge Barr finally appeared. On his arm, Morgana Barr looking more ravishing than before. He introduced her to the few who did not already know her and then asked that everyone be seated. A minute later, he reappeared.

"Gentlemen," he glanced at his daughter and smiled, "and *lady,* our guest of honor." He stepped aside and Lee Morgan looked up . . . astonished. There stood one of the most notorious man hunters in the west. A man who rivalled the likes of Hickok, Holliday, Earp—even Kit Carson. "Meet, if you please, Mister Tom Horn."

Small talk consumed much of the meal. Morgan entering into only a minor exchange.

"I'd heard you were dead, Mister Horn." Horn looked across the table, smiled and nodded. He finished chewing, swallowed and then took a swallow of wine.

"I heard the same damned thing 'bout a week back as I recollect. Can't be though. Not a word in the papers about it." Everyone laughed.

Horn was not a big man. Maybe five feet, eight or nine inches and 165 pounds. His hair was cut short and he wore a well groomed moustache. His face appeared somewhat leathery, years, Morgan supposed, of exposure to the elements. Big or not, Tom Horn's reputation was as big as Sawtooth Mountains. He was the last of a breed of men being devoured by the undertow of advancing civilization.

Horn was not a shootist in the sense of Frank Leslie or Hickok, though his skill with a handgun was considerable. It was storied that he had once won a shooting match down in Omaha. The first half of it lasted until noon. Twenty-two competitors were eliminated. It was near dark before it ended—Horn against William F. Cody. True or not, few men could rival Horn's skill with a rifle and he was reported to be as icy cold as a Bowie blade when it came to killing a man.

"Mister Horn," Judge Barr finally said, "everyone in this room knows why they're here and why I sent for you. You told me you had a plan. Would you share it with us?"

"Put a man on the inside," Horn said. "Best way . . . and by far the safest . . . to kill a Grizzly is to track 'im home. Next time he goes out, stay put and catch 'im comin' back."

"The only man who could do that, sir, would be

yourself." Horn shook his head. "Too many folks
know me. A passle that I've never laid eyes on.
Nope. Has to be somebody who can show cause for
wantin' to join up and a reputation to back it." Horn
sat back, picked up a table knife and pointed it at
Lee Morgan. "Frank Leslie's boy. Sure got the reputation and there's enough old tales about Leslie's
rivalries to make it work . . . mebbe."

"I'm here as a favor to the judge . . . to listen."

"Funny . . . Judge tol' me he reckoned you'd help
out after what happened over in Boise."

"I'm not your man. I've got a score to settle . . .
and I'll settle it, by myself."

"Lee . . ." Judge Barr said. It was as far as he got.
Tom Horn stopped him cold.

"You've got a problem young feller. See, if you're
runnin' around out there settlin' accounts . . . an'
me, I'm working for the ranchers . . . settlin'
accounts, well . . . it occurs to me our trails would
have to cross."

"Likely, Mister Horn."

"Then . . . I'd have to kill you. I get a mite edgy
man huntin'. Judgment's not what it was twenty
years ago. I'd feel bad . . . real bad. I'd even say so at
your buryin'."

"I don't like threats, Mister Horn," Morgan said.

"Oh now don't take me wrong, son. I'm not
threatenin' you. No sir. What I related, that there's
just the way it is. Seems to me we'd do better by one
another—an' for these folks here—if we'd work together."

Morgan couldn't disregard the man but he was
not without a reputation of his own. "You seem
pretty certain of the outcome of any meeting we
might have, Mister Horn."

"I'm downright positive," Horn said. "I've heard

about your gun hand. I'd guess you probably would give your own daddy a fair run . . . an' that makes me appreciate you 'cause I *saw* him." Horn scratched the back of his head and cocked it sideways as he finished his conversation. "Thing is, I'd prob'ly kill you from half a mile away. Fast gun don't do a man good at that distance."

"Seems like a good plan to me," one of the other men said. "Morgan there on the inside and Mister Horn on the outside. Sounds like we'd find out what we need to know." Others nodded and mumbled agreement but there was a tension in the air. Morgan finally dispelled it.

"I'll sleep on it," he said.

Morgan was awakened by the sound of what he thought was thunder. It proved to be a dozen riders in the front yard of the Rocky Barr. His first thought was a raid but the voices he heard soon relieved that fear. He slipped on his britches and shirt, stuffed the Bisley into his waistband and headed downstairs. Tom Horn was just ahead of him.

"What's the ruckus?" Morgan asked. Horn shrugged. They found Judge Barr on the front porch along with Morgana and one or two of the ranch owners who'd opted to stay the night. One of them was a man named Ben Strada.

Strada's spread was half again the size of the Rocky Barr. It was named for the area in which it was located, the Lost River. Strada had four sons, two nephews and a niece living with him. His own wife, her brother and his wife had all perished when a bridge gave way during a treacherous storm five years earlier. They were swept to their deaths in the Lost River.

The riders who had come so late were some of
Strada's men.

"Boss . . . they hit us. Same night you pulled out."

"My God! The family . . . what of . . ."

"Your niece boss . . . they took your niece. They
burned one o' the bunk houses and a toolshed but
nothin' else. It was almost like . . ."

"Like *what*, man, spit it out."

"Like they come after her." Strada turned to his
host. Judge Barr had never seen Strada look so pitiful, so helpless.

"You've got my payment . . . more if the others
won't join us. Do what has to be done. I want my
niece alive . . . safe and I want those bastards strung
up." The judge only nodded.

"Your niece, Mister Strada . . . how old is she?"
Strada turned and was looking into the face of Lee
Morgan. "I've changed my mind. I'll work with you.
I'll get inside their gang . . . if I can."

"God Bless you, Mister Morgan. She's twenty-
five . . . just three months ago. Her name is Lileth."

Tom Horn had walked into the yard and was
talking with Strada's men. A few minutes later,
Strada came back out of the house, fully clothed.
His horse was waiting. He mounted up and then
turned to the men on the porch.

"I'm going to start hiring men . . . any kind I can
get, at any price. When you get inside, when you
hear something, I want to know. Then, I'll be
ready." Strada spurred his horse and the thunder of
hoofbeats echoed again at the Rocky Barr and then
faded.

Back inside, Judge Barr, Horn and Morgan gathered in the study. Soon, Morgana served coffee.

"Strada's upset," Horn observed, "but he's
making a mistake hiring outside guns."

"I'm not sure I follow you," the Judge replied, "after all, Mister Horn, *you're* an outside gun."

"A professional. I won't sell out on you to the next man who offers me more. I'll finish the job I'm hired to do and if I don't, you don't pay."

"I agree, Judge," Morgan said. "We could end up having to face in both directions. The kind of men Strada's likely to get won't give a damn about who's who. If they can collect on one of your men . . . or Killerman's . . . they will."

"I'll try to talk to Ben later. He's usually got a cool head." Horn turned to Morgan. "Where do you start? Boise?"

"Uh uh. I had a run in with the law in Boise . . . Grover too."

"You've been a busy man, Mister Morgan."

"But it might come in handy. Let the word get back to both places about me. Tell 'em I came lookin' for work . . . you offered it and I turned it down."

Horn grinned. "Just ridin' in to get a look at the place."

"Maybe somebody will think so." Morgan turned to the judge. "I'll have to describe your place in detail . . . the whole layout. There's a helluva risk in it, Judge."

"What have I got to lose? I'm only biding time now. Do what you have to do, Morgan."

"What about you, Mister Horn?"

"Figure it's time you start callin' me Tom. What's your likin'?"

"Morgan will do just fine."

"Well," Horn said, "I figure there's two groups o' these bastids. They've hit ranches too far apart in two short a time just to have one outfit."

"I'll go along with that," Judge Barr said,

shaking his head, "but where in God's name do you start looking? It's a big country Horn."

"I was talkin' with Strada's foreman. That outfit hit the ranch from the northeast. There's a dozen or so smaller ranches in that area and then Killerman's place. I figure one batch o' these buzzards is holin' up along the Bitterroots."

"You know that country?" Morgan asked.

"Not real thorough."

"I used to hunt some of it as a kid. Lived close by for awhile. Use Taylor Mountain for a landmark. Follow the Salmon to its confluence with the Lemhi. That'll take you into one of the most remote regions of Idaho. Goes on for miles. Hunters used to go back fifteen, twenty miles. Never talked to anybody went back all the way. There's a cut . . . solid rock on both sides and the farther you go . . . the deeper it gets. They call it Gunsmoke Gorge."

"Sounds likely Morgan. What about you?"

"I agree, Tom, that there's likely two batches of raiders. I'll mosey over to Picabo. It's a meeting point for about every gunny riding through the territory. If I get anywhere I'll have a good chance there."

4

A cold, drenching rain had been falling for the last three hours. Morgan had the collar of his oil cloth slicker pulled up around his neck, his hat pulled well down on his head and he hunkered low in the saddle.

Mostly his thoughts had been with big Ole' Thomassen. The old Swede either knew *something* or saw *someone*. In all of the previous raids, there had been no reports of any of the victims searching out possible perpetrators. Ole' seemed to know where to go and who to look for. Not that it did anyone any good now.

Pacer, Morgan's big dappled gray, snorted. Morgan looked up. Light! Picabo. He rode in, eyeing buildings on both sides of the single street. There were fourteen buildings in Picabo. Six of them were empty. The decent folk had long since departed. There was a mercantile, a smithy and livery stable and an assay office. Their existence did not necessarily reflect the honesty of their proprietors. The balance of Picabo's business district consisted of four saloons and the Acey-Duecey. It was a hotel, brothel and saloon combined.

Morgan stabled Pacer, threw his bedroll and possibles over his shoulder and toted his Winchester in his free hand. The outside doors of the Acey-

Duecey were closed . . . the bat wings tied open, against the chill. Morgan entered and looked around. A dozen or so men were scattered throughout the saloon. Some drank and talked, four were busy with poker, others mingled with the girls . . . three of them.

There was no registration desk so Morgan walked to the bar. He dropped his gear to the floor and slipped out of his slicker.

"Got an empty?"

"Two dollars a night or eight fifty a week. Food's separate. Eat down here. We got no room service." The grimy looking barkeep grinned. "Least ways for food."

"I'll start with two nights," Morgan said. He payed, took his key and went straight to his room. The furnishings were sparse. A bed with a lumpy, straw filled matress, a three drawer dresser, a washbowl and pitcher and a chamber pot. There was a single window which gave the occupant a view of the roof of the building next door.

Morgan pulled back the bed covers and saw no signs of life. He didn't like bedbugs and had learned to tote his bedroom with him . . . just in case. He slipped his knife out, slit a footlong gash into the end of the mattress and slipped the winchester into the slot. He was using the chamber pot when he heard the knock at the door. It came a second time before he'd finished. He slipped the pot back under the bed and opened the door, stepping back as he did so.

"Water señor and towels." Morgan eyed the Mexican boy and then looked passed him into the hallway. Morgan nodded and the boy came in. He filled the water pitcher from a bucket. "I am Jose, señor." He turned and smiled. "Jose Delgado

Manuel Ruiz Esteban. If I can do anything for you, señor. Just call me."

"I'll do that," Morgan said, "but I think I'll stick with Pancho. You mind being called Pancho?"

"No, no, señor. That was my padre's name. Pancho Aguilar Esperanza . . ."

"Okay, Pancho," Morgan said, holding up his hands. "There is something you can do for me." Morgan held up a silver dollar. "Are there any . . . uh, *gringos* in Picabo? I don't mean like me . . . gun men. I mean rich type, *Yanqui gringos?*"

"No señor."

"You're sure?"

"Si. Jose," he grinned. "I mean . . . Pancho, he would know."

"Have there been any such men . . . recently?"

"No señor . . . no such men come to Picabo." Morgan nodded and flipped the silver dollar to the boy. "*Gracias amigo.*" Morgan held the door and Pancho took his leave. He had his doubts about Pancho's credibility but he also thought it likely that the best he'd get in Picabo was contact with a hired gun . . . no one really important.

Morgan made his way to the bar. He noted as few additional customers but none of them appeared to be much more than second rate gunnys and a grifter or two.

"Whiskey," Morgan said. The barkeep poured. Morgan downed the shot and nearly gagged. "That's the most god-awful whiskey I ever drank. You got better?"

"Nope."

"Beer?"

"It's green."

"I'll take it." The barkeep shrugged. Morgan heard the door and did a half turn to see who came in. It was a man. A pinch-faced little fellow in an ill-fitting suit and a derby. He was carrying a large, fancy leather case. He looked around the room and finally found Morgan. His eyes dropped to Morgan's rig. He smiled and walked toward the bar.

The barkeep brought Morgan's beer. He took a long swallow. It was green. It was still better than the whiskey.

"Good evening to you, sir." Morgan nodded. "My name is Mason sir, Andrew Jennings Mason. If you have a few minutes, I'd very much like to show you my wares." He held up the leather case.

"Not interested," Morgan said.

"Ahh sir . . . that is where you are mistaken. I assure you, just take a look and give me a few minutes and you will be."

"Why'd you pick on me . . . uh . . . ?"

"Mason, sir."

"Uh huh. So why?"

"By my reckoning, sir, after years of experience I might add, I'd wager you earned your keep with that Bisley Colt's. Not another man in here is wearing as fine a pistol."

"You're a gun drummer?"

"I am sir . . . with the finest manufacturer in the country . . . Smith and Wesson."

"I've never owned anything but a Colt's."

"And a fine weapon they were too, yes sir, fine weapons," he smiled, "in their day."

"But you've got one better?"

"I have, sir, I have indeed." He pointed to the case. "In there reposes the beginning of a line of firearms which will take this nation into its new century. It is the pistol of civilized man. A weapon which will maintain the law which Mister Colt established with his legendary Peacemaker."

"You want a beer, Mister Mason?"

"Why yes, sir, that would be fine."

"You get us a table," Morgan said, "and I'll get us a beer. I'll take a look see at your fancy piece."

If the pistol handled and fired the way it looked, Morgan would have to concede to the drummer's sales pitch. Nickled, beautifully hand tooled engraving and gutta-percha grips.

"Double action, six shot, five inch barrel, .38 caliber."

"I prefer something a little heavier," Morgan said, hefting the pistol. "Heavier caliber too."

"Look here, sir." Mason handed Morgan a metallic cartridge with a somewhat bulbous shell. "When that missile strikes its target, it flattens out. It will, putting it bluntly sir, tear a hole as big as a man's fist upon exiting."

"Well Mister Mason, I won't say I'm not impressed but I'm just not in the market for a new gun right now."

"Nor are most men of your ilk," Mason said, smiling. "You are my most difficult sale because you demand much and are loyal to a fault. Therefore, sir, if you will but sign this simple form, I will present this weapon to you along with holster and ample ammunition. I'd like nothing better than to place it in your hands for what my employers refer to as a field test."

"You want to *give* me that pistol?"

"In a manner of speaking, yes sir. I live in Boise, Mister Morgan. After using it, I'd like you to look me up and let me know, honestly, what you think. Anything we discuss thereafter will be determined by your interest."

Morgan frowned. "You know my name?"

"Oh yes," Mason said, standing up and folding up

his case. "By now, most everybody in Boise knows your name and what you look like." Mason pushed the pistol and ammunition boxes across the table. "Good day, Mister Morgan, and good luck to you."

Mason went upstairs and Morgan was puzzled. He got the answers to his questions when, later that evening, he opened the first box of ammunition to load up the new pistol. There was a handwritten note inside the box.

> Mason is a friend. He stopped by the ranch and I asked him to help. I told him where you were and what to do. Good luck.
>
> Judge Barr

The rain had stopped. The clouds still hung low and the wind gnawed its way through a man's clothing and chilled his bones. Morgan hurried out of the Acey Duecey following his breakfast and over to the mercantile. He'd gone to see Mason early that morning but the drummer had already checked out.

Morgan was wearing the new Smith and Wesson. He'd pulled it a couple of dozen times in the privacy of his room. It seemed to increase his speed but he had an empty feeling without the weight of the big Bisley.

Inside the store, he lingered by the pot-belly, warmed himself and took stock of his cash. He had about fifty-five dollars. He spent just under fifteen of it on a new, sheepskin coat. He was not in New Mexico now.

"You're Lee Morgan aren't you?" Morgan had just pocketed his change from a twenty dollar bill. He looked up at the man behind the counter.

"Who wants to know?"

"A friend of mine," the man said. He motioned with his head and indicated a doorway to the back of the store.

"I'm staying across the street. If your friend is interested, that's where I'll be."

"I'm interested." Morgan looked up and found himself staring into the business end of a scatter-gun. "Why don't you step this way, Mister Morgan?" Morgan shrugged.

In the backroom, Morgan found himself in company with four men. One continued to hold a shotgun on him. The others were seated. Two of them were well dressed but they all wore either shoulder holsters or hip rigs.

"What brings you to Picabo?" The man who asked the question had his chair leaning back against the far wall. Morgan could see the shoulder holster. Morgan thought the man looked like a Pinkerton agent.

"Passing through," Morgan said.

"To where?"

"East."

"Where east?"

"That's *my* business."

"You shot up two of my men, Mister Morgan . . . in Boise. I don't like things that cost me money. They did. A lot of it."

"My mistake," Morgan said.

"That's hardly restitution. Why were you so interested in defending an old Swede sod-buster?"

"A friend of a friend. Nothing personal."

"What friend?"

"Belle Moran."

"Are you usually that impetuous?"

"They hardly gave me a chance to get their side of

the story," Morgan said. He unbuttoned the heavy coat. One of the other men moved forward in his chair and Morgan detected a shifting movement by the man holding the shotgun.

"What's your game, Morgan? You pistol whipped the sheriff and already crossed swords with the territorial marshal. Or so I've heard. Then you try to save some farmer as a favor to a Boise whore." The man smiled. "You are an enigma, Mister Morgan."

"I'm a man who keeps his business to himself and appreciates it when everybody else does the same."

"But you *didn't*," the man replied, standing up now. "You stuck your nose in *my* business. You owe me Morgan . . . at least an explanation."

"After which you nod at shotgun over there and I get my nice new sheepskin coat all pocked up with bird pellets."

The man pulled a cigarette case from his inside pocket, opened it, removed a cigarette, offered one to Morgan, who declined, closed the case and replaced it in his pocket. He lit the cigarette, took a long drag, savoring the smoke, exhaled and then said, "I could have ordered you shot anytime. Why do you suppose I didn't?"

"I've got something you want . . . or you think I do."

"Are you on Judge Barr's payroll?"

"I'm not on anybody's payroll."

"But you do want to find out who burned out the Spade Bit, don't you?"

"Why should I?"

"Because it was your home . . . or what passed for it." The man smiled. "If you tell me you're not that old shootist's son . . . old Leslie, well then Morgan, our little talk is over."

"Yes," Morgan said, "I'm Leslie's son and I did

live at the Spade Bit ranch once and, yeah, I'd like to find out who burned it down." Morgan smiled. "I'd buy the son-of-a-bitch a drink."

"That so? Why is that?"

"I rode back up here to settle accounts with the folks who lived there. Somebody saved me the trouble."

"What account did you have to settle. They owned it legal and proper, didn't they?"

"They did. It's *how* they got it that bothered me."

"I don't follow."

"Easy enough. A retired gun fighter moves in. Got a son who doesn't exactly stay within the law. Not neighbors you'd invite to Sunday dinner. On top of that, the law was never quite able to pin old Frank Leslie down . . . or his son. Judge Barr sure tried enough times. Anyway, when old Leslie finally got his, the son stood to inherit the place. A simple change in a deed here, a little shuffling of papers there and pretty soon, Leslie didn't own the place anymore and his son has got nothing to inherit but a lousy reputation."

"You sound . . . shall we say, bitter."

"Not as bad as it was. Not after I saw the Spade Bit. The thing with the old Swede was just like I said. Fact is, I thought the old bastard might have some information for me. He used to work for Judge Barr."

"So," the man said, grinding out his cigarette beneath his boot heel, "you'd like to see the same thing happen at the Rocky Barr as happened at the Spade Bit?"

"Yeah . . . only I'd like to do it personal."

"Can you prove that," the man said, whirling to face Morgan, "or are you really not what you seem?"

"I don't have to prove a damned thing to anybody." Morgan had carefully eased back the hem of the skeepskin coat. The new pistol was at the ready.

"Prove it to me, Morgan, and I'd make it worth your while. You'd get that chance at the Rocky Barr. You could ride out of Idaho a lot wealthier than when you rode in."

"So you're the fella that engineered the destruction of the Spade Bit?" Morgan smirked. "The other ranches too, huh?" He smirked again. "Real nice work, yes sir. Rocky Barr still stands, Josh Killerman's Rocking K still stands and Ben Strada's place."

"They're big spreads . . . hard to get at but . . ." Morgan had hit a nerve. The man's response was quick, defensive. Obviously he wasn't the biggest fish in the stagnant pond and he was getting some pressure from someone. Morgan decided to push . . . hard.

"But you figure they'll all buckle under now because some dumb son-of-a-bitch stole Strada's niece." Morgan forced a laugh. "That . . . when they could have had old Judge Barr's daughter for Chrissake!"

"Daughter?" Morgan's play got the desired reaction. "Judge Barr's daughter is in . . ."

"San Francisco? Jeezus," Morgan said, sneering, "who the hell you got workin' for you, blind men? Morgana Barr is out at her daddy's ranch right now. Oh you may get some folks stirred up with your move against Strada, but you move against Judge Barr and you'll get action." Morgan moved his right arm so quickly no one in the room had any warning of his intent.

Morgan himself was astonished at his own

increased speed. The lighter, short barreled, Smith and Wesson was pointed right at Morgan's target. He smiled.

"You won't ride out of Picabo alive."

"Neither will you," Morgan said. "Now get that scatter gun off of me and clear these half assed slingers out of here. Maybe then," he continued, giving his most sinister grin, "just maybe, you and I might do some business."

Moments later, Morgan and the man were alone. "I'm Jake Lambert," the man volunteered.

"I want ten thousand dollars, Mister Lambert, and that's just for what I know. How to get into the Rocky Barr and how to get hold of the judge's daughter. I can supply the same information at Killerman's place. When it's all over . . . when your people have control, I want the rest."

"The rest?"

"Ten percent."

"You're crazy."

"Who says so . . . you? That might irritate me a little Lambert except I know you're not the top man."

"And how do you know?"

"You didn't engineer the Strada kidnapping and you people can't be in two places at once. Besides Lambert, your end of things isn't going too well right now. The biggest thing you've managed is the Spade Bit. . . which is nothing as long as the Rocky Barr is standing."

The man turned. Morgan saw a look which displayed both concern and embarrassment. "I can tell you now, Morgan, ten percent is out of the question. You may have information of value but we'd still have to act on it . . . you couldn't do it alone. That's why you're in Picabo."

Morgan sat down. He pondered Lambert's observation. In fact, he was killing time until he could play the ace he held. He looked up. "That ten percent bother you 'cause it's more than you're getting?"

Lambert was caught short. Here was a man who was more than the two bit, fast handed son of an old time killer. "No . . . no it *isn't* more than I'm getting."

"You don't think it would be worth another ten percent to your boss to get this thing over with in a hurry . . . and before you start losing riders."

"We haven't lost a man yet, except for the two you got. That won't happen again."

"It damned near happened tonight right here in this room, Lambert. I can assure you, it'll start happening in a big way shortly." Morgan could almost read Lambert's thoughts. "You can backshoot me . . . it won't stop what I just told you. What I know has already happened . . . all hell's about to bust loose in Idaho." Lambert was whipped and Morgan knew it.

"I've got to . . . to talk to my people."

"Why? You and I can deal. We make some moves on our own, get them done and then you talk to your people. By then they'll have felt the sting and will be ready to deal. There's more here than ten percent— for both of us."

"You're talking a double-cross Morgan. You don't know who I'm dealing with . . . you . . . you don't understand."

Morgan had him on the run. No double-cross? Then the action wasn't all local. Morgan moved to play along.

"Okay . . . then let's just make ourselves look too good to be ignored. As much as there is at stake,

I've got to figure somebody would be willing to pay plenty. It's heating up. The army will be in on it eventually. Right now, it's a civil matter with a handful of lawmen to deal with it. Most o' them can't catch cold."

"All right. . . what's your plan?"

"You sleep on what I told you, Lambert. Think on it hard. We meet again. I want a deal . . . a solid deal. Give it to me and I'll deliver." Morgan got to his feet. "Fuck with me, Lambert . . . and I'll kill you."

5

Lee Morgan's plans were pretty simple—if they worked. They were dangerous as hell if they didn't. When the time was right, he'd produce Judge Barr's daughter and suggest that she be taken to the same spot where Strada's niece was being held. That, he figured, would lead him to the top man. If he got that far, he'd reveal the presence of Tom Horn. The combined information ought to solidify his position.

He had plenty of time to ponder the possible outcomes. Some of them, he thought, were none too pleasant. Neither was the ride from Picabo back to Grover. The rain of four days had turned to snow. The wind, down from the Sawtooth, piled it up against every break. Morgan couldn't remember the last time he was so glad to see the lights of Grover.

He stabled Pacer and payed extra for a rubdown and top quality feed. He walked toward the Sawtooth saloon, hoping he wouldn't be seen by any old acquaintances and hoping the gun drummer, Mason, had managed a message to Judge Barr. He knew he didn't dare ride to the ranch again but he would have to try to make contact with either the judge or Tom Horn.

"Whiskey," Morgan said to the bartender. He wasn't the same man Morgan had seen on his first day in town. "Leave the bottle. I've got some warmin' up to do."

"Which way'd you ride in?"

"West," Morgan lied. He was also wondering about the marshal. "You got law here?"

"Marshal's got an office but he's not in it most o' the time. Rode out two days ago for Boise. Doubt he'll be back too soon with the kind o' weather we got." Morgan nodded. He was relieved.

After another drink, Morgan shed the sheepskin coat and found an empty table. He'd been seated for only a few minutes when two men entered the Sawtooth. Morgan knew they spelled trouble for him. They were the two riders he'd used the Black snake on, the day he'd ridden up to the Rocky Barr. They glanced around but missed seeing him. Both were stomping their feet, knocking off snow and blowing on their hands to warm up. A moment later, they walked to the bar.

Morgan had learned from Judge Barr that the taller of the two was Milt Ryker. He was a drifter, better than average with a six-gun and a shade too hot-tempered to hold any position of responsibility. His saddle compadre was Billy Creek, a nonentity whose sole claim to fame rested on his dubious reputation with a pistol.

"What brings you boys all the way down to Grover from the Barr?" Ryker responded. "Lookin' to hire some hands. Figgered they might be a few loafin' around after what happened down at the Spade Bit. Seen any?"

"Few. Fact is, a fella rode in tonight," the barkeep said. He leaned to one side so that he could see around Ryker. He frowned. "Hell . . . he was settin' right over there." The barkeep pointed, Ryker and Creek both turned but they never got all the way

around. Both spotted Morgan just as he reached the
door.

"That's the son-of-a-bitch with the bullwhip,"
Creek shouted. Creek and Ryker both were wearing
long, heavy coats. Ryker had his clear of his hip
first, but Creek was in his line of fire. He pushed
Creek to one side, planning only to get the drop on
Morgan. Too much happened too fast.

Morgan whirled, in a crouch. The Smith and
Wesson again proved its worth. Ryker took a slug in
the chest which shattered his sternum and dis-
tributed the bone fragments into both lungs and his
heart. The bar held him up for a moment, then he
slid down, slowly, dead by the time he'd attained a
sitting position.

The bartender dived for cover almost at the same
instant Billy Creek made his move. He'd cleared his
coat and made his draw but he never got to fire.
Morgan turned the little S & W on a flick of his wrist
and Creek took the .38 through the head. Just then,
the door opened behind Morgan. He turned and
found himself face to face with one of Lambert's
men. He'd been reasonably certain he was being
followed from Picabo. If what had just happened
was inevitable, it couldn't have happened at a better
time.

Morgan turned back, addressing himself to no one
in particular. "Anybody asks questions . . . just tell
the truth. It'll save me looking for you later." He
holstered his gun, turned, stared for a moment at
Lambert's man, half smiled and walked out. He
made his way, quickly, to Sarah Browning's
boarding house.

Sarah was a fine looking woman. Solid, tall but
not lacking feminine attributes. She had once
cooked out at the Spade Bit and had nursed

Morgan's father through more than one bout with ailments.

Morgan's thrice failed efforts to settle down had been highlighted by an association with Sarah. They'd gone to town dances and picnics together and she'd even managed to get him into church. He'd never managed to get her into bed. He'd often wondered if that had finally driven him back to the wild life—a conquest he couldn't claim.

"Hello Sarah." It was dark. She squinted.

"Lee? My goodness! Lee Morgan?" He nodded. "Come in out of the cold." He did. She took his coat and he sat down and tugged off his boots. He remembered Sarah's fetish about clean rugs.

"I need a room."

"I have one. How long . . . *this* time?"

He stood up. "It's good to see you again," he said. She didn't pursue her question. "Am I too late to get something to eat?"

"Of course you are," she said, then she smiled. "Bacon and eggs do?"

"And a little coffee."

Lee took a seat at the kitchen table while Sarah flitted about preparing his food. "When did you get back?"

"A while ago."

"I suppose you heard about the Bit?"

"I did. I shot two men at the Sawtooth," he blurted out. "Just before I came over here. It was self defense."

She turned and gave him a pitiful look. She shook her head. "Isn't it always?"

"It is with me," he said.

She smirked. "Your father too . . . as I remember him talking about it. They're no less dead . . . are they?''

"I wanted you to know. Nobody will come looking
for me ... unless it's the marshal. I figure to be gone
before he gets back from Boise." She didn't respond
but rather returned to preparing his food. When it
was ready, she put it before him, poured two cups of
coffee and took the chair kitty-cornered from him.

"Smells damn good," Morgan said, smiling.

"You know Lee, they've got horseless carriages
back east. Electric lights and trolley cars and inside
water closets. You carry a gun and ride a horse and
shoot men down in barrooms like some pulp novel
villain."

"Good," he said, between bites. He washed them
down with a swallow or two of coffee. He wiped the
corners of his mouth. "If I was going blind ... would
you want me to cover my eyes up right now ...
tonight ... or let it happen when it happened?''

"You're such a damned child," she said, angrily.
"It's the kind of answer I would expect. My God!
Take off that damned gun and settle down. *I* live in
this country. The people who board with me live in
this country ... we don't go around shooting people
... self defense or not."

Lee mopped up the egg yoke with his last crust of
bread, folded it and slipped it into his mouth. He
washed it down with the last of the coffee and then
slid the cup toward Sarah. She refilled it.

"No disrespect intended," he said, "but you don't
live civilized because there is civilization. You just
ignore what's going on around you ... let somebody
else make it right. I came back to see about buying
back the ranch. You know what I found. It didn't
happen just here. There are violent men out there
and Mister Edison's lights and a few noisy street
machines aren't going to stop them."

"Men like you . . . like your father . . . you won't give up, will you? You won't admit that your time is over. Somehow you seem to think you'd be less a man if you ran a general store or taught school. They have violent men back east too but citizens don't go about gunning them down. There are laws, law men, courts and judges. It's a requirement of a civilized social order."

"And someday it'll get here to Idaho. West too. It will happen when those greedy men who take what someone else has worked for, are made to understand they can't do it out here anymore than they can back east."

"I don't want trouble under my roof," Sarah Browning said. "You can stay the night." She got up, hastily cleared the table and started for the upstairs. Morgan caught her arm.

"I'm sorry about your husband. I heard."

"It changes nothing between us," she said. "I don't want anymore hurt."

She pulled free of him. "Please . . . don't make me ask you to leave." Morgan looked into her eyes and nodded.

Lee Morgan woke himself up . . . a habit he'd long since mastered . . . about 2:30 the following morning. By now, he concluded, the Sawtooth was closed and Lambert's man would be fast asleep. It was the one opportunity he might have to get a message out of Grover and into Judge Barr's hands.

He dressed, slipped quietly downstairs and eased out the front door. The snow and wind had increased and struck him like the slap of a hand. He sucked in his breath and tucked his chin against the thick, wool collar of his coat.

At the livery stable, Morgan had a hard time rousing old Ben Grafton. Grafton was none too pleasant when he finally responded to the incessant pounding at his door.

"You got 'ny idea what the fuck time it is?"

Morgan handed Ben a sealed envelope. "Your boy takes that up to Judge Barr for me *now* and brings me back an answer. There's a hundred dollars in it."

Ben stepped back and invited Morgan inside with a toss of his head.

"Must be goddamn important."

"A hundred . . . by the end of the week."

"Fifty now," Grafton said, "fifty when he gets back."

"You've got my horse. I won't be leaving. Hold him 'til you get your money."

Grafton grinned, exposing short, dingy teeth. "Bullshit! You can steal a goddam horse Morgan . . . you've done it before . . . and worse."

"Then hang onto my saddle . . . it's worth fifty."

"Like I said . . . must be awful important. How's come you don't ride it in?"

"I've got a man to meet. I miss 'im and neither one of us will get payed."

"Sattidy," Grafton said, "by noon . . . or I got a saddle *an'* your horse."

"You get the money when I get Judge Barr's answer. Faster Luke rides the faster he gets back." Grafton nodded and Morgan returned to Sarah Browning's.

Dawn came to the Bitterroots as brittle as dry bread. The sky was clear and the air seemed frozen in place. Tom Horn snuffed out the last of the coals from his fire and scooped cow dung over it. The dung had been fresh a few minutes earlier. Now it was cold. In ten minutes, it would be frozen solid. It stopped the smoke from trailing too high.

Horn saddled his mount, double checked the tie downs on his pack mule, checked the loads in his Sharps and his Henry and mounted up. He rode back down the slope and onto a rolling meadow. He reached the Lemhi River and turned to follow it . . . south.

By mid-morning, he'd reached the spot where the river took a sharp bend back to the west. Here is where he'd leave it. He turned east and began the slow climb that would take him to the tops of Medicine Ridge. The spiny outcropping tailed off to the southeast and eventually ran headlong into the granite wall of the Continental Divide.

Somewhere in between, he'd find the entryway into the area known as Gunsmoke Gorge. Horse and mule were at a walk. Tom Horn had just bit off a chew. He'd been obliged to slip the tobacco under his armpit for twenty minutes to soften it up. He tucked the chunk back into his coat pocket. It was then he heard the shots! There were three but just exactly their point of origin was tricky to discern. Horn reined up and cocked his head. The reverberations continued. His mount snorted. He patted the mare's neck. The mule balked. Horn nudged his horse ahead, taking up the slack in the tether line.

Another shot! Straight ahead . . . no doubt. Horn raised up in his stirrups, shoved his hat back, shaded his eyes with his free hand and scanned a hundred and eighty degrees. Off to the left, he saw what he wanted . . . a stand of trees. He rode toward them.

A small stream, ice forming along its banks, meandered through the grove. It left his animals with both grazing and water. He tied them short . . . about twenty feet and hobbled both. He removed his heavy coat, rolled it up and slipped it between the

ties on his pack mule. He undid a bundle and
removed a shortwaisted, wool and cotton wind-
breaker.

Working at a slow but carefully practiced routine,
Tom Horn removed a leather case from his pack
mule. He pulled a box of ammunition from his
saddlebags, checked his pistol load and then opened
the leather case.

Inside was Horn's magnificent, customized man
killer. A Remington Creedmoor, .44-90. The rifle had
been manufactured for quick dismantling or
assembly. Its 32 inch, octagonal barrel, machine
threaded for a fitting to a pistol grip stock.

Horn wiped the light moisture from the weapon,
assembled and loaded it. He replaced the case,
shoved his hat down more snugly against his head
and set off along the creek.

About a quarter of a mile away, he crossed the
creek and climbed a razorback ridge which he
followed for another mile. Soon, he had a view of the
open valley below. He'd found what he'd wanted. A
line shack used for summer round-ups . . . now
presumably abandoned. This one was not.

There were three horses tied outside and he could
see a deer laying near the front door. He guessed the
animal was the victim of one or more of the shots
he'd heard earlier. Horn guessed that the line shack
either belonged to the Strada spread or the
Killerman ranch. Either way, it was remote from
both and afforded the marauders a place to hole up .
. . or, he mused, a place to stash a kidnap victim.

The door opened, Horn tensed. He shifted his
weight and hefted the Creedmoor to his shoulder.
He steeled himself against the recoil, positioned the
barrel and took aim. A man—then two—stepped
outside. One of them knelt beside the deer. They

were talking.

Suddenly, a third man appeared. Horn lowered the rifle and rubbed his eyes to remove the excess moisture. He squinted. Yes, he thought, it is . . . it's Ben Strada. The three men talked for several more minutes. Finally, Strada disappeared back inside. The others strung up the deer. Strada reappeared and was carrying a woman's hat. He and the first man mounted up, exchanged conversation with the third man and then rode off to the south. The remaining man began gutting the buck.

Tom Horn pondered what he had seen as he made his way back to his horse. Had Strada's men found the girl? Had they stumbled into the marauders? or had Strada received a message and made a deal?

Horn didn't repack the Creedmoor. He mounted up and started toward the line shack, cradling the weapon in his arms. Horn began to think back on the incidents which had led him to the remote area. Strada's men suddenly appearing. The story of a raid and the kidnapping of his niece . . . but no serious destruction to his place. Thus far, according to Judge Barr, no ranch had escaped the fury of the raiding band. Why, he wondered, had Strada's? How did the gang know exactly when and where to hit? Strada had more than fifty good men working for him.

The line shack was in view. A ribbon of white smoke curled up from the single chimney. The deer was gutted and all but stripped of hide. The man was not in sight. Horn dismounted, tethered his horse to a fallen log, made a quick survey of the terrain and began walking down the hill.

Horn had halved the distance to the shack. The snow had deepened and the going was tougher. Suddenly, the man appeared from the opposite side of the building. He spotted Horn at once. Perhaps a hundred and seventy-five yards separated the two, but the man obviously didn't want company. He drew and fired his pistol!

"It's Tom Horn." Tom stopped. The man darted inside. The old man hunter waited, once again positioning the Creedmoor. There was no window on his side of the shack. The man reappeared, rifle in hand.

The first shot was fifteen or so feet in front of Horn. The second, closer but off to the right. The man wasn't taking his time. Tom Horn did. He sighted the Creedmoor until its barrel levelled out on the man's chest. The third shot struck a log just three feet from Horn's legs. Horn squeezed the trigger.

The .44-90 barked and Horn's whole torso rocked from the recoil. The shot itself was sharp and clear but it boomed against the nearby ridge, bounced off and spread out over the snow. Even before the sound had faded, the man in front of the shack was hit. The force lifted him from his feet and hurled him backward, spreadeagled, into the snow. His rifle burrowed into a nearby drift, barrel first. The man didn't move.

Horn heard the whinny of the man's horse, now tied on the opposite side of the shack. The horse settled down. Horn waited. He could hear nothing else. He moved cautiously toward the shack.

The shack was empty but there were ropes—or pieces of ropes—around the rungs of the back of a wooden chair. They had been cut. Someone had been tied to it. Horn moved outside and examined the man. Most of his chest and back was pulp. Horn went through his pockets.

A kerchief, two expended rifle shells, a piece of

chaw and half a sack of makings. There was no indication of who the man was and Tom knew he hadn't been among Strada's riders.

Nearly three miles away, Ben Strada pulled his mount up short. "That was a rifle!"

"Yeah," the other man said, "sounded like a Sharps." Strada frowned. "Get back to the shack . . . check on Owens and look for tracks. I'm going on over to the Killerman place." The man nodded. He'd ridden only a few yards when Strada hollered at him.

"Yeah?"

"You see anybody you don't know," Strada said, "don't take any chances. Kill 'em!" The man nodded.

6

Sarah Browning changed her mind. Lee Morgan could stay with her as long as there was no trouble. By late morning on his third day in Grover, there hadn't been.

That aside, Morgan was getting edgy. Today was the deadline for the deal he'd made with Ben Grafton. Morgan hadn't seen anything of Grafton, his son or Lambert's hired gun. No news wasn't good news. On top of that, Morgan knew the marshal was due back almost anytime.

When he answered the door, he found Sarah Browning holding out an envelope. Somebody had come through. "I'll be movin' out today," he said, "one way or another."

"It's just as well. I don't like old ashes stirred up." Morgan smiled. "If there are no coals," he said, "what difference does it make?" She walked away without responding. He watched her descend the stairs, then he opened the envelope.

Sawtooth saloon. Upstairs.
1:30 today.

Lambert

Morgan rolled the makings, lit up, set fire to the

note and watched it burn itself away in the washbowl. The shot spider-webbed the mirror above the
chiffonier and Morgan dived for the wall just below
the window. Behind him, downstairs, Sarah
screamed.

Another shot smashed through the window. By
the angle of the shot, the shooter was in the house
next door . . . or on its roof. Morgan heard the creak
of a board in the hallway. He fired two blind shots
out the window, tucked his body into a ball and
rolled toward the bed. The door flew open and
Morgan fired.

The man's reflexes managed to pull one of the
triggers on the shotgun. The blast tore out a chunk
of the ceiling a foot across. Morgan's shot was fatal.
Instantly, he was on his feet, propelled himself over
the man's body and down the stairs.

"Are you all right?" he yelled. Sarah was standing
in the archway between the hall and the parlor,
hands cupped to her mouth. She just nodded.

Morgan went out the front door, took a sharp
right turn and saw a man darting around the corner
of the house next door. He cut between the houses
and made for the protection of a huge elm tree. A
shot tore bark from it. Morgan wheeled and fired. It
was the first good look he'd had of his antagonist.
The man pumped another round out of the Henry
and then turned and disappeared into an alleyway.
Morgan backed against the tree and reloaded.

Morgan kicked down the door of the room above
the Sawtooth saloon. Lambert was sitting on the
edge of the bed. Another man leaped to his feet from
a chair. Morgan slammed his fist into the man's jaw
and sent him reeling. Then, he leveled the pistol at
Lambert's head.

"What the hell is this all about?" Lambert's question carried audible concern and a fearful expression.

"I warned you in Picabo," Morgan said. He eyed the man he'd hit, just now shaking off the blow and trying to get to his feet. "He makes a move, you're my target, Lambert."

"I want to deal, Morgan. That's why I'm here. That's why I sent you the message."

"Followed with two gunnys . . . only they came up short."

"I swear to Christ, Morgan, they aren't my men."

"How about the man you work for, Lambert, can you speak for him too?"

"I can. I mean . . . he doesn't know anything about you. I simply told him that I had a plan that was worth more to him than Strada's niece. He gave me five days, Morgan . . . five days to deliver. Jesus! There are gunnys riding into Idaho from every direction. Those men could have worked for anybody—even the law."

"You going to deny you had me trailed?"

"Hell no . . . but my man saw what happened at the Sawtooth . . . you forget that? I know those men worked for Judge Barr. That's what convinced me that you were telling the truth."

Morgan considered Lambert's position and his words. They made sense. He looked at the man on the floor. He put both hands out and shrugged. Morgan stepped back and slowly holstered his weapon.

"Sit tight, Lambert, and tell me your deal."

"You produce Barr's daughter and bring her to Ketchum. You've got four days to do it . . . all of it. I'll have a man waiting for you. His name's Pete Walker. He'll lead you from there."

Lambert moved his hand toward his coat. Morgan drew. "Easy . . . I've got your money. All of it . . . ten thousand." He pulled a thick envelope from his inside coat pocket. He smiled. "See . . . I trust you."

Morgan took the envelope and slipped it into his pocket. Again, he holstered the S and W. "The only thing I don't like so far, Lambert, is your man. I meet *you*. *We* do the dealing."

"You didn't count the money. I figured you trusted me."

"You figured wrong. If it's not all there I'll come looking for you and I won't be so damned accomodating the next time."

"Damn it! I've got things to do . . . preparations to make so that we . . . you and I . . . get the most out of this that is possible."

"Then," Morgan said, smiling as he backed out the door, "you'd best get started. You've only got four days."

Big Ben Grafton was hauling horse feed when Morgan showed up at the livery. He jammed a pitchfork into a bale . . . hard. "I was just thinkin' about you son. You begun to be a worry to me."

"You got my answer?"

"Depends."

Morgan pulled the envelope from his pocket, rifled the bills and withdrew two one hundred dollar notes. "Your boy's money and a hundred for taking care of my horse and forgetting that you saw me today."

Grafton snatched the money from Morgan's hand. He smiled. "Don't push your luck, Grafton."

"You don't scare me none, gun man. That pistol won't help you none while I'm bustin' your ribs." He smiled again. "I figure mebbe that there message was worth a whole heap more'n a hundred."

"Don't try to run a bluff with me," Morgan said. "I picked you and your boy for the job because neither of you can read." Grafton frowned and then assumed a surly expression.

"You callin' me and mine dummies?"

"On the contrary, I knew you'd be smart enough to keep the deal to yourself. Why take a chance on losing it all?" Once again, Morgan's lightning-like right hand produced the pistol. He pointed it at Grafton's head. "The answer," Morgan said, "right now!" Then he smiled. "And tell your boy to come down out of the loft . . . real slow and careful. If he gets careless . . . you'll be the first to pay for it." Grafton's jaw dropped. "Tell him . . . *now.*"

Morgan had Grafton's son ready his gear and saddle Pacer. Then, he sent the youth to Sarah's house to fetch the rest of his belongings. Ben Grafton produced an envelope and handed it over to Morgan.

> I've left the appropriate orders with my men. You won't have any trouble on the RB and Morgana will be waiting. Nothing yet from TH. May God ride with you.
>
> Isaac Barr

It was snowing again by the time Lee Morgan and Morgana Barr reached the eastern boundary of the Rocky Barr ranch. It had taken Morgan three full days to ride up from Grover, make his way to the area on the ranch where Morgana took her daily ride and pull off the bogus kidnapping. By midnight of that third day, they had reached the last of the Barr's line shacks.

"We'll get out of the cold, eat and spend the night," Morgan said. "We should get to Ketchum by noon, if we get an early start."

Morgana prepared rabbit stew and even baked biscuits once they had warmed up. Morgan made certain the mounts were out of the weather and then the couple ate . . . mostly in silence. Afterward, with a cup of hot coffee, Morgan rolled a smoke.

"Would you do me one of those?" He looked up, surprised. She smiled. "It's quite common in San Francisco. At least among the young women. Do you find it that shocking?"

He considered her. She was strikingly beautiful and there was nothing artificial about her. He couldn't help but let his eyes roam the form beneath the buckskin, low cut top and the shapeliness of legs, emphasized by the form fitting riding breeches.

"Takes quite a lot to shock me," Morgan said.

"But that doesn't answer my question."

"No . . . I don't find it shocking." He handed her the cigarette and then held out a match. She took a long drag, leaned her head back and let the smoke seep from pursed lips. It hung in a blue haze just above her face.

"My father would," she said, looking again at Lee. He didn't get her meaning. "Find it shocking, I mean."

"Yeah . . . I'd guess he would."

"He'd find a lot of things shocking about me. San Francisco isn't Idaho. It isn't folksy little dances on Saturday nights at the local Grange hall." She sipped her coffee and then licked her lips, slowly, provocatively. "Have you ever been there?" Morgan shook his head. "You'd like it."

"Mebbe . . . but I don't like feeling cooped up . . . hemmed in. I think that's what I'd feel."

"Not if you were with the right person." Morgana suddenly slid far down on her chair and thrust out her right leg. She held it up. "Would you mind," she said "my boots?" Morgan ground out his cigarette, eyed her and then took hold of the tall, black riding boot. It came off . . . hard. The left was worse and he ended up on his ass on the floor. Morgana laughed. Morgan just grinned, sheepishly.

It might have been the horses stirring or the howl of a wolf. Either way, Morgan was awake instantly and holding the little Smith and Wesson. The fire had nearly died out and the cold was invading the shack. Morgan sat quietly on the edge of his bed just listening. Now, there was nothing but the wind off the Sawtooth and his own breathing.

He'd been staring at the floor. He looked up. There before him, silhouetted by the remaining glow of the fire, was the upside down "V" of Morgana Barr's legs. She reached out and took his face in her hands. She bent from the waist and kissed him. Her tongue darted between his lips and she lowered one hand, found one of his and lifted it to a bare breast. The nipple hardened under his touch. She stood straight again.

"Why," Morgan asked.

"Why not?" she replied. She had spread a buffalo robe on the floor near the fire. She moved to it, dropped to her knees and then slowly lowered herself down. She took the poker and stabbed at the coals. They sparked, popped and briefly flared into a small flame.

The light played across the creaminess of her stomach and the dark patch below it glistened. Lee Morgan was in no mood to question her further. He slipped out of his britches and long-johns and walked to her. He looked down.

"I like to see the man who's making love to me," she said. He shoved a large log into the fireplace and

prodded it into position. Soon, it caught and the
flames swelled up around it. Morgan knelt between
Morgana's legs, lowered his torso and began licking
her breasts.

Morgana's breath was soon coming in short, rapid
gasps. Her fingers dug into the robe and she
undulated her hips beneath Morgan's groin. He
continued to lick, pausing, alternately, at the pink
tipped summits of soft flesh.

"Gawd . . . it's been so long . . . so very, very
long," she cooed. Her hands found her own thighs
and rubbed their insides. Her body stiffened with
the delight of it. Morgan went lower . . . lower still.

Morgana Barr climaxed almost instantly . . . but
she showed no signs of wanting Morgan to stop. He
didn't. His tongue worked in and out of her most
intimate recesses, pausing only at the most sensitive junctures or in response to the girl's reaction.

He glanced up. She was fingering her nipples and
even thrust the tips of her fingers into her mouth to
moisten them . . . transferring it to the sensitive
buds. His own passions had built to their peak and
he now covered her with himself and carefully
guided his swollen shaft, inch by inch, inside her.

"Slowly," she said in a whisper, "do it slowly . . .
make it last." Morgan complied, pumping with a
controlled rhythm on which he had to concentrate.
He licked at her ears, nibbled at her neck and then
raised up enough to slip his hands over her breasts.

Suddenly, she began to respond. It wasn't slow. It
wasn't controlled. It was a frenzy of unleashed
emotion. She moaned, cried out and thrust her hips
so hard against his own that there were even
moments of pain. He raised up so that he could take
total control of the depth and speed of the activity.

"I'm . . . I'm . . . oooh . . . Jeezus," she cried.

Morgan now thrust against her and they were pumping together. It was, finally, together that they reached the ultimate moment, the blending of man and woman, body and soul. Their nakedness crashed against the buffalo robe in a final burst of lust and then they lay, quiet, content—spent.

Ketchum, Idaho was a barely organized pile of kindling wood in a valley of the Sawtooth Mountains. Between Picabo to the south and Stanley to the north, it was the only respite from untold acres of wilderness.

It was a winter haven for the permanent employees of two score of small ranches. There were three saloons which doubled as bawdy houses, a livery, general store, stage station and, of all things, a church! The latter was the domain of one Ephram Gregory Culpepper. He was a hell-fire and damnation bible thumper who claimed to be a prophet of the first order. He'd been known to shoot a man or two who'd questioned his dubious credentials.

It was to Parson Culpepper's church that Morgan rode when, just after noon, he and Morgana rode into Ketchum.

"Stay mounted," Morgan told her. He trudged through the two feet of snow and pounded on the door. A woman opened it. Her hair was stringy, much of it pulled back, tight, against her head. She wore a long, high-necked, black dress. There was no sign of cosmetics on her face and she displayed a perpetual frown.

"Who dost thou seek?"

"The parson," Morgan said. "Mister Culpepper." The woman stepped back and Morgan entered. She closed the door behind him and he followed her into a small room, obviously the parson's study.

"Sit thee here . . . and wait," the woman said. She exited the room, closing it off behind her. Morgan peered out. Morgana remained on her horse. He felt a little guilty. It was cold and beginning to snow again.

Morgan's head turned to the sound of the sliding doors and he couldn't hide his reaction to Ephram Culpepper. The preacher could have passed for kin to Abe Lincoln. Tall, gangly, gaunt of features. His face was framed in an inch wide, inch long, black beard . . . a horseshoe shape which was trimmed to a fault. Only one feature of the man set him apart from the likes of Lincoln or any man of God Morgan had ever seen. Tied down low on his left thigh was a black holster. In it reposed a Colt's .45 Peacemaker. Culpepper smiled when he saw Morgan's eyes fall upon it.

"It's my proof to the doubters and the sinners of the world," Culpepper said. "It is spoken of in the Good Book."

"A gun?" Morgan frowned. He was no Bible scholar but he'd read some and heard aplenty.

Culpepper grinned, perhaps at his own interpretation. "Blessed are the peacemakers," he quoted. "For they shall be called the children of God."

In a flash, Culpepper's long, slim fingers curled around the butt. He moved with the precision only practice can bring. He displayed the Curly Bill spin, the border shift, three fast draws and ended by flipping the weapon into the air, catching it after a two and a half twist and holstering it. "I can shoot with the same precision," he said dryly. "If I salvage no souls, I am at least assured of their undivided attention and I am free of hecklers."

"I'll remember that," Morgan said, clearly

impressed. He glanced again out of the window at
Morgana. Then he said, "I am given to understand
that you know why I'm here." Culpepper nodded.
"You'll take the woman in?"

"I will . . . and you can feel safe about her."

"Yeah . . . I feel a hell of a lot better about leaving
her here than I did before."

Culpepper reached into his inside coat pocket and
withdrew an envelope. "I've written the letter as the
good judge asked. It will verify Miss Barr's
presence and states that she will be released upon
receipt of the appropriate sum. Also in the envelope
is Judge Barr's own letter to me . . . for your own
verification."

Morgan read both, looked up and nodded. "If I
get what I want . . . a meeting with the top man, I'll
get word to you."

"And if you don't?"

"No plan, friend," Morgan said. "Use your own
discretion."

"Mister Lambert *is* in Ketchum . . . Addie Terhune's place."

"You know for sure?"

Culpepper nodded. "I know. I know Lambert.
Shot up two of his men one time."

Morgan smiled. "Wouldn't attend services?"

Culpepper wasn't smiling. "Beat up one of
Addie's girls . . . real bad. Didn't want to crawl back
on their hands and knees and apologize and then ask
for Divine forgiveness. I saw to it they got another
chance . . . face-to-face with their Creator."

"You a friend of Adele Terhune's?"

"Am now," Culpepper said. "Used to be her
husband . . . twenty years ago. She is what she is
because of me. I left her destitute. Now . . . I'm
working off the debt."

"A Bible-thumping gun slinger," Morgan said, shaking his head in wonderment, "you really believe Jesus would have done the same?"

"Don't know," Culpepper replied, scratching at his beard thoughtfully. Then he smiled, "But he had a dozen men working for him that I figure would have."

"You're my kind of preacher, *Reverend* Culpepper," Morgan said. "I'll be in touch."

The ride to Addie Terhune's saloon and whorehouse was a short one but Morgan felt better than he had in several days. He knew now that Morgana would be safe and he was in a position to make demands which would, almost certainly, get him on the inside.

Culpepper knew whereof he spoke. Lambert and two gunnys were ensconced in Addie's best room. Morgan eyed the two men with disdain and Lambert dismissed them with but a nod of his head.

"Where's the girl?"

"Safe."

"We had a deal Morgan."

"Had is right," Morgan replied. "Things have changed." Lambert was livid. "I can offer more than just the girl . . . and I want in on the action against the Rocky Barr . . . direct!"

"You son-of-a-bitch! I stuck my fuckin' neck out a long ways for you." Lambert was on the verge of trying Morgan. Morgan knew it. He shoved the sheepskin coat away from his hip. Lambert's fingers were flexing. Morgan smiled. "I don't deliver . . . we're *both* dead men."

"Uh uh," Morgan said, pointing with his left hand at himself, "not me. I can deliver . . . and right now Lambert . . . what I can deliver is a helluva lot more important to your boss than you are."

"Look," Lambert said, relaxing his fingers and sounding more pleading than angry, "I told . . . uh . . . my people that I'd deliver a bigger fish than Strada's niece tomorrow. Hell . . . even if I *wanted* to deal with you there isn't time."

"There's time. You're less than a day's ride from your people." Morgan took off his coat, sat down and began to roll a smoke. "I can deliver Morgana Barr within six hours. I want in for the raid on Barr's ranch . . . another ten thousand for the additional information I've got and the ten percent we talked about."

Morgan spit out a loose piece of tobacco, wet his lips and lit the cigarette. He looked up at an astonished Jake Lambert and added, "And I want to meet the top men . . . here."

"You're fucking crazy Morgan. I've got enough men to handle you. You might get some of 'em . . . but you can't get 'em all. The answer is *no!*"

"And what's your boss gonna say about that?"

"Nothing," Lambert replied, grinning. "He'll never know anything except what I tell him. That'll be that you tried a double-cross and I had you killed."

"And when he finds out the truth?"

"He won't."

"The hell he won't. Damn near any man you've got working for you would sell you out in a heartbeat for the right money and I've got the *right* money. Ten thousand, Lambert. You gave it to me yourself."

"You rotten bastard!"

"Relax, Lambert. I'm not crossing you. I'm just sweetening up the pot for both of us. Play the hand," Morgan said, "you've got a sure draw to an inside straight and you're in too deep to fold."

Jake Lambert made one, final, pathetic plea to Lee Morgan. "Damn it Morgan . . . there just isn't time. I'm most of a day's ride from my contact. He expects me to ride in there with the girl late tomorrow. I can't ride in without her."

"You could if you rode in early . . . like tomorrow morning."

"Now how in the hell am I going . . . to . . . do . . ." Bullshit! It's snowin' like a son-of-a-bitch out there . . . and cold. Goddam it . . . I'm not leavin' tonight. Tomorrow's ride is bad enough."

Morgan shrugged. "It's up to you," he said.

Morgan stood up, butted his cigarette and slipped on the sheepskin coat. He walked to the door, opened it and then turned around. "I'll be downstairs . . . at least 'til midnight. If you change your mind, let me know. If not I'll do the next best thing."

Morgan was half way through the saloon, wondering if he had pushed too hard. A man . . . any man, could only be pushed so far. Jake Lambert had been pushed since the day they first met and Lee Morgan had done all the pushing. He'd learned first from his father and then from first hand experience, that being surprised in a fight could be fatal. He thought he'd gauged Lambert correctly. But what if he hadn't.

He looked up at the poker table to which he was headed. The man on the far side of the table glanced at Morgan and then his eyes shifted to a spot just above Morgan's head and behind him. The man started a movement to his right, off his chair.

"Jeezus!" the man shouted. Morgan's right hand moved like the bull whip and came up with the S and W. He crouched, spun to his left and fired. He was only shooting from the memory he had of the stairway. He fired a little low.

His shot struck Jake's gunny in the groin, traveled upward, obliquely, and severed his spine. He fell forward, over the bannister and somersaulted through the air, landing on the end of the bar . . . dead! A half a dozen pellets from the shotgun ripped into Morgan's left coat sleeve. Two of them pierced coat and shirt and longjohns. Morgan felt the sting against his flesh.

The second man's shot took Morgan's hat off. Morgan killed him. The .38 smashed into his chest, dead center. The door opened and Ephram Culpepper stepped inside, ducking a little to do it. Morgan saw him draw and fire just left of Morgan's position. There was grunt and then a body toppling over chairs and crashing to the floor. Culpepper holstered the Peacemaker.

"Let he that thinketh he standeth take heed lest he fall." Morgan turned. One of Lambert's gunnys lay dying. A man Morgan had never seen. "Addie overheard the gentlemen upstairs planning your untimely end," Culpepper said. "One of her girls came by to let me know about it."

"I owe you," Morgan said.

"A small contribution to my humble ministry will suffice." Culpepper's eyes then shifted to the balcony. Addie Terhune was standing there and pointing down the corridor. Morgan holstered his gun and went upstairs.

"You're all alone, Lambert. I told you to play out the hand. Too bad. Now you're out of the game." The door opened and Lambert stepped into the hallway. He had both hands in the air.

"We can still deal," he said. "I . . . I got scared. I'm dealing with powerful people. You'd understand if you knew them. Jeezus Morgan . . . please . . . I know I can't take you . . . I know it. Just give me a chance to ride out. I can still make the deal . . . just let me ride out.''

Lee Morgan had been in the spot before. He knew the outcome already. He even knew how it would come about. He backed up to the stairway, turned and started down. Jake Lambert made his move. He was pretty good. He was also scared and he was much too fast to be accurate. Morgan killed him.

7

Tom Horn had decided to get himself warm and have a cup of coffee. Why waste a perfectly good line shack and a hot stove? Besides, he had some figuring to do. Strada's niece had obviously been held in that shack. Strada had been there only minutes ago. Horn was deeply disturbed by that turn of events. He'd seen it before. The big land company . . . or the railroad . . . or whoever . . . finally gets to someone inside the ranch owner's association. Was it Strada?

Then again, Horn knew it could be almost anyone in the group. Nearly every man would have the opportunity to get onto Strada's ranch and kidnap his relative. It would certainly keep the attention off of them . . . or at least most men wouldn't look for an inside connection. But Tom Horn wasn't most men. He had the distinct feeling that Lee Morgan wasn't either.

He heard the horse snort. Someone was back. He grabbed the Creedmoor, leaned his chair back against the wall for support and waited. The door latch lifted. He heard the man outside shift his weight and cock his pistol. He'd shoot first, Horn thought, and worry about whom he'd shot later. Horn pulled the Creedmoor back until the butt plate rested against the wall. Then he pulled the trigger.

The .44-90 took out a chunk of the door the size of a dinner plate. The old, rotting wood just splintered. Most of it was driven into the man's chest and abdomen. The slug from the Creedmoor did the rest.

Horn sat in the silence after the reverberations of the shot had died away. He listened. There was no sound. He opened the door, moving slowly, carefully. The snow in front of the shack was a dirty pink. The man's face was frozen into a quizzical expression. Horn stepped over his body and found the tracks where he'd ridden in. Two sets of tracks headed south . . . only one set coming back.

He returned, knelt down and removed the man's hat. It had partially covered his face. "I'll be goddamned," Horn said, aloud. "Toby Summers." Horn studied the man's face . . . a confirmation of his first belief and then he looked south. "There's suthin' *big* afoot," he said.

He pushed himself to his feet with the Creedmoor as a crutch. He stood it against the wall of the shack and commenced to bring the men's bodies inside. That done, Tom Horn headed for his mount. Whatever was going on . . . it was south of where he was and he intended to find out.

Of all the puzzlements to date, the appearance of Toby Summers was the most disturbing to Horn. Summers had a reputation as one of the best bounty hunters still alive. He didn't work cheap when he worked at all. In recent years, that had become more common. Many states now outlawed bounty men and rewards being payed were far below what they had been in the mid eighties. Mostly though, Summers had made a habit of never working for an organization . . . only a man . . . one man and Summers had to be certain that his employer was

the top man. Either he'd softened with age and
grown careless or he was working for Ben Strada.

The break in the trail was clear enough for a blind
man to follow. A single set of hoof prints trailed off
to the southwest. That would be Ben Strada. Tom
Horn studied his map of the country. About eight
miles distant was the Killerman Ranch, the Rocking
K. The other set of tracks veered east and a little
north. A wagon . . . not heavily loaded and pulled by
only one animal . . . and a rider on horseback.

Horn stood up in the stirrups and took a slow, half
turn of the horizon. Nothing unusual. He sat back
down, took a final glance toward the Killerman place
and then turned east. First things first and he was
looking for Gunsmoke Gorge . . . not Ben Strada.

Tom Horn's eyes scanned ahead constantly. He
was riding in the open. He didn't like it. He stopped
several times to get his bearings. He was grateful,
finally, when he saw the stream called Leadore.
Once he crossed it, a stand of trees paralleled the
tracks he was following. He'd have some cover.

The pack mule bellowed, the tether line grew taut
and Horn's mount dug in, whinnied and then
balked. Horn still cradled the Creedmoor and as he
slipped from his horse, he freed up the Winchester.
The sickening sound of an arrow burying itself in
flesh now reached his ears. The mule toppled over. A
second arrow already protruded from the animal's
side.

"*Whhewt . . . thunk!*" His horse reared. Horn
could see the arrow in the animal's neck. In a crouch,
Tom Horn darted for the opposite bank of the creek.
The skimpy shelter it provided was limited to a
boulder or two.

Two more arrows assured that Tom Horn would
walk from this place, if he got away from it at all.

The water was icy cold . . . knee deep. He would not long be able to stay in the water. Far across the creek in the tree line where he'd hoped to find some cover, he saw movement. One man . . . two. For sure . . . two.

"Horn," he whispered to himself, "b'lieve you got yourself in a tight." He looked in both directions. Behind him there was a creek wash. It led back northwest and into some trees. Thing was . . . it was better than 150 yards to the wash . . . all open ground.

The ricochet of the rifle bullet off the boulder just inches above Tom's head, answered the question he'd been asking himself. Did his pursuer . . . or pursuers, have anything other than bows and arrows? Another shot was closer. A third spattered rock chips against his coat. It had come from a different angle.

"Two it is, Tom," he said, "an' in a minute, them fellas is goin' to have you in a crossfire." A few feet from him, he spotted a snagged tree limb. He eased toward it. Another shot was way off the mark. Both men were re-positioning. Tom freed up his Bowie, slit a hole in his denims at about calf height. He slipped a sturdy part of the snag through the hole. He let his weight fall back . . . pulling on it. The denim ripped a little more . . . then held.

A rifle shot hit the water in front of him and he heard the bullet beneath its surface. He wedged the Creedmoor down beside him and then pumped a round into the Winchester's chamber. Another shot from his front side struck the rock, chipping it. He felt grains of sand strike his cheek.

Now, Horn slipped the Winchester between his knees, tested the water's depth, nodded, smiling and picked up the Creedmoor. A shot came from behind him. It was close . . . too close. He turned, hefted the Creedmoor and fired a round at nothing. He ducked down. None too soon. Another shot struck the boulder which, a moment before, had been hidden by his head!

Tom pushed with all his strength against the creek bottom. He went staight up and then backward. The Creedmoor flew from his hand and landed, ten feet away, in the water. It gurgled out of sight. Tom landed on his back and disappeared. The current tugged at him but the snag and the denim britches held. His upper body floated to the top until his face was out of the water. The only other thing above the surface was about two inches of the Winchester's barrel.

"Sure givin' that water proofin' elixir o' your'n a test, Mister Winchester," Tom said to himself. A moment later, he heard legs splashing into the water from in front of him.

"I think I got him," the man yelled.

"You'd better make sure." The splashing stopped . . . thirty to forty yards. Tom tilted his head forward slightly. He could see a man. He was dressed in buckskins and a buffalo coat. He was raising a rifle to his shoulder. Tom Horn pulled with all his strength against the snag. He submerged. The shot, deflected by the water, ripped into his coat just at the collar. He could feel the pull but no pain.

"I just made sure," the man yelled.

There was splashing in the water behind him. His lungs were tightening. The rifle was totally submerged. He couldn't risk the shot. He pulled again with his leg and struggled, underwater, to free himself from the snag. The splashing in front of him was very near. Tom Horn opened his eyes. He could see leather boots.

The man was upon him. Tom stood straight up, coming out of the water with an old Indian yell and sounding like a banshee. He swung the Winchester like a sledge-hammer, full from behind him. The stock cracked and so did the man's skull. Tom went forward . . . back into the water, face down.

"Son-of-a-bitch!" The voice was behind him. Tom grabbed the man's rifle as it entered the water and then rolled to his left, struggling to regain his footing. He struck a rock and felt a sharp pain on the back of his head. He pulled his knees up to his chest and pushed.

Two shots entered the water where Tom had been. He reasoned that one or both of them must have struck the body of the other man. Tom came out of the water and fired three shots from the Henry in rapid succession. Two of them struck their intended target. One in the shoulder, the other in the side. The man went down.

Tom Horn dragged the wounded man from the creek, hog-tied him and then went back to the water. He retrieved his weapons and then dragged the first man's body from the water. He knew he'd have to move fast if he was to keep from freezing to death.

The wounded man was white. His companion had been an Indian or at least a half-breed. Horn was lucky to be alive. The man was now howling for help. Horn ignored him. The wounds would freeze shut so the man wouldn't bleed to death. At least he'd live long enough to tell Horn a few things.

Horn unpacked his gear, lugged it to a clearing about forty yards into the trees. He knew it was risky, but he had to build a fire. He did. He stripped out of his half frozen clothing, got himself dry and put on plenty of dry, warm clothing. He unloaded all his weapons and broke them down to dry their working parts.

Those things done, he went back and carried the wounded man over by the fire. "You're a dead man, son, so you might as well tell me what I want to know. You an' your friend have horses."

"God mister . . . please . . . please. There's a doc. He can save me. *Please.*"

"A doc?"

"In the camp. Six, seven miles." The man coughed. He'd warmed some and the bleeding had started again. "Our horses are tied south—about half a mile back. Jesus! You can't just let me die."

"This camp," Horn said. "Is it called Gunsmoke Gorge?" The man nodded. "Who do you work for?"

"Oh God . . . please mister . . . help me."

"Talk to me, son . . . if you want relief."

The man nodded. "I don't know the big boss . . . just the ramrod. Name's Brock." The man coughed and winced. The bleeding in his side was profuse. "That's . . ." he coughed . . . "that's all I know, Mister."

Tom Horn looked up at the sky. It would be dark in less than an hour. He still had the horses to find. He knelt beside the man, cut open his shirt and examined the wound in his side. It was bad. If he could get quick medical attention, he would live. Otherwise, he'd bleed to death.

"I can't take you to that camp," Horn said, standing up. "I'd get killed. You wouldn't make it on your own and it's too damned far to the Killerman spread. I got no doctorin' supplies with me for anything that bad." Horn turned, picked up the Henry the other man had been carrying and walked back to his prisoner.

"Mister," the man coughed, "God . . . what . . . what are you gonna do?"

"Recognize that I can't help you and try to remember that you tried to kill me . . . you no good bastard." Tom Horn pulled the trigger.

Addie Terhune kicked on Morgan's door. "Got some breakfast for you," she shouted. A moment later, Morgan opened the door. While he washed his face and finished dressing, Addie prepared a place to eat. "You didn't fare so well last night, did you?"

" 'Bout three hundred . . . give or take twenty dollars one way or the other."

"You usually that bad at poker?"

"If I was," he said, smiling, "I'd damned well quit."

"Well, better luck next time." She started for the door.

"I don't like eatin' alone . . . I get plenty o' that."

"I've had breakfast . . . two hours ago."

"How about some coffee?"

"And some *answers*," she asked, smiling.

"You got'ny?"

"I doubt it."

"You mind bein' asked?" She shrugged. Morgan ate his eggs and a slice of toast washed down with two swallows of coffee. Then he looked up. "What do you know about what's going on in Idaho?"

"It's bad for business . . . sometimes anyhow. I get plenty of customers . . . from both sides . . . but mostly . . . I get trouble just like ever'body else."

"That it?"

"That's enough. I'm not buyin' more trouble than I already got, Mister Morgan."

"You got as big a stake in this as most ranchers. Why not?"

" 'Cause I'm not rooted like them ranchers. I can move on to any two-bit cow town around. Minin'

camps too . . . or lumberin'." She smiled. "Men are
the same no matter what they do for a livin'."

"No names . . . no faces . . . no locations?" Morgan
considered her. He went back to eating and waited
for a reply. He got it.

"Nope."

"Then tell me about the preacher."

She laughed. "The Reverend Mister Culpepper.
Reason he's a preacher is 'cause o' the fact he's
already been damn near ever'thing else. Not worth a
tinker's damn at any of 'em . . . 'ceptin' for shootin'.
Now at *that* . . . there's not too many better."

Morgan finished his breakfast and poured more
coffee.

"You want that coffee spiced up a bit?" He
nodded. She slipped a hand under her dress, lifted it
to her thigh and revealed a small, silver flask. It was
held in place by a garter. She took off the lid and
poured half the contents into Morgan's coffee and
the other half into hers.

"I thought women like you carried a knife or a
Deringer in that spot." She raised the dress again,
lifted up her other leg and Morgan saw the Deringer.
His eyes trailed above the gun. She grinned.

"That's not for sale anymore."

"What kind of a man does it take to get it?"

"One I like," Addie replied, "an' it takes me
longer to figure out if I like somebody than it used
to."

"Anything special you look for?"

"Yeah . . . one that don't ask too many questions."

"You helped the other night. Was that for Culpepper?"

"That was for Addie Terhune. I don't like Lambert . . . that is . . . I didn't. I don't like anybody
gettin' backshot . . . an' I don't like others gettin'

the idea that this place can be used for their personal business . . . good, bad or otherwise."

"Can you trust the preacher?"

"If he likes you . . . yes."

"He don't know me that well."

"He's not doing it for you . . . he's doing it for the judge."

"Then you *do* know."

"I know he's helpin' Judge Barr. I don't want to know anything else." She got up. "I've got work to do."

"I'm obliged for the breakfast."

"Don't be . . . it'll be on your bill."

It had been three days since Morgan's confrontation with Jake Lambert. He'd concluded that someone would come looking. Now he was beginning to wonder. He was also wondering about Morgana Barr but he didn't expose the connection with Culpepper more than it had been. Just after noon, another knock came at his door.

"Yeah." Morgan had his pistol leveled at one of the panels, about belly high.

"Miss Addie says to tell you there's a man in her office who wants to see you . . . a gun drummer."

Addie let Morgan in and then took her leave. "Mason," Morgan said, smiling, "before anything else, I'll tell you now that your Smith and Wesson is a fine piece."

"I knew you'd find it so, Mister Morgan. Later . . . we'll settle accounts." Morgan nodded. "I've a message for you." He handed Morgan an envelope and then walked to the door.

"Hold it, Mason. You been to the ranch?"

"Good afternoon, Mister Morgan." Mason walked out. Morgan was angry. He opened the door to yell at Mason but thought better of it. After all, he didn't know who else might be in Addie's place. He closed the door, ripped open the envelope and read.

> I appreciate what you and others have tried to do. I really believed if we banded together we could stand against these men. I know now that we cannot . . . and the risks are too great. Please return at once with my *property.*

>   Isaac Barr

Judge Barr buckling under! Morgan couldn't believe it. No man he'd known, save for his father, had been stronger and more principled then Judge Isaac Barr. He read the note again. He sat down. Perhaps Tom Horn had learned something, he thought. Or perhaps the judge was just too concerned for Morgana's life.

"Damn!" Morgan was up against something he hadn't often had to face. He didn't know what to do. The door opened. It was Addie Terhune and she looked scared!

"Addie?" Suddenly, she was shoved inside the office. Behind her, two men appeared from either side of the door. Both were leveling shotguns at Morgan. He started to get up.

"Stay put," the first man said. He stepped inside, looked around quickly and then re-focused on Morgan. The second man was whispering to a third. In a moment, he entered the office as well and shut the door behind him.

"We've got a bit of a wait," the first man said, "so the lady here can pour us all a drink." The second man moved to Morgan's side and relieved him of the S and W pistol. Two minutes later, the door opened again and Mason stumbled through it. Behind him, a third man.

Before anyone could say anymore, a fourth man came into the office. He was well dressed but armed with a cross-draw style, waist belt holster.

"Morgan, I'm Harv Jessup. You killed four men who worked for me. Jake Lambert was one of them. That was very costly, very costly indeed. Nonetheless, I was told you could do something for me. If what I heard was true," he smiled, "then I would be of a mind to forget all about the cost. I'll ask you just once. Is it true?"

"I talk to the top man." One of the men holding a shotgun slammed the stock into Morgan's back between the shoulder blades. He groaned and went to his knees.

"I'll tell you now, Morgan, the next time I want him to use that shotgun, he'll use the other end. You're as high as you're going to get . . . at least for now."

Morgan got to his feet. He pulled his shoulders back and flexed his back muscles to ease the pain. "It's true," he said.

"You've got the girl?"

"I've got her."

"Where?"

"Now, Mister Jessup, you've gone as high as you go." Morgan smiled. "At least for now."

"Don't make the mistake of pushing me, Morgan. I'm not Jake Lambert."

"Exactly," Morgan said, "and that makes the difference between the real value of my participation and the double-cross that Lambert planned."

"Double-cross?" Jessup considered Morgan. "You telling me that Jake Lambert double-crossed you?"

"Not me . . . you, Mister Jessup. And whoever else is involved. I've got brains enough to figure out that I'm not up against a few cheap guns . . . and I'm not that greedy." Morgan sat back down, leaned back and feigned complete relaxation. "Why don't I tell you everything and then you tell me what it's worth?"

"Yes, Mister Morgan, why don't you?"

"The rancher's association hired a man killer—a professional. I'm not talking about a gunny. I'm talking about a *hunter*. A man who stalks his prey and kills him and moves on. He'll chip away at you." Morgan grinned. "My guess is that he's already started."

"And you know who this man is?"

"I do . . . and pretty much where to find him."

"How?"

"Mister Mason here. He's my contact with the ranchers." Morgan eyed Mason. He could see Mason's fear, but all he could do was hope that Mason would play along. "That's why he came to see me this morning . . . to let me know the whereabouts of the man the association hired . . . and to collect."

"Collect?"

"His pay. Five thousand."

Jessup looked doubtful. "That's a lot of money, Morgan. Just who was going to pay him?"

"*I pay him*," Morgan replied, "it's . . . well, call it an investment. I'll get it back."

"From where . . . or should I say . . . from *who*?"

"Either from you and your people or directly from Judge Barr."

"All right, Morgan. Who's this man killer?"

"Tom Horn."

Jessup was incredulous. "That's just a name," Jessup finally said. Morgan knew the man was fishing and trying to maintain a composure he didn't feel. "Can you prove that?"

Morgan chuckled. "Everyone of you damned people ask the same question. Lambert asked me what I could prove too." Morgan got to his feet.

The man behind him, holding the shotgun, stepped forward. Jessup held up his hand. Morgan glanced back at the shotgun man. He grinned. He turned back to Jessup. "I've got Judge Barr's daughter . . . you've got Ben Strada's niece and I know where Tom Horn is looking. Which of those things do you think will bring the most results, Jessup?"

"Where's he looking?"

"You want it *all* from me, don't you?"

"You've got the girl. She's your security." Jessup smiled now. "Unless you're lying."

"But you already know I'm not," Morgan said. "That's the reason it took you three days to contact me. I've got her and Tom Horn is snooping around up in the Bitterroots." Morgan could see the slightest change in Jessup's demeanor. Although he hated to run the risk of Horn being found, he'd have to play out the charade.

"A well hidden gorge, Jessup. Folks hereabouts call it Gunsmoke Gorge."

"You're guessing."

Morgan laughed. "That's a marked improvement, Mister Jessup. A few minutes ago I was a liar. Now I'm a guesser. You forget," Morgan said, "I was raised in these parts. I expect I know the country about as well as any man . . . better'n most . . . sure as hell better'n Horn. Now eventually, he'll sniff you out. Whole thing is for somebody to find Horn before he finds you."

"And that somebody is you. Am I right?"

"I want three things," Morgan said. "I want the chance to ride with you when the Rocky Barr is taken out. By my reckoning, the judge will buckle under to save his daughter. I want a third of the ransom money."

"And what do you want for taking out Tom Horn?"

"Whatever the rancher's association was paying him . . . and the reputation for the job . . . whether I do it alone or not."

"That's all?"

"That's two. The Rocky Barr and the ransom go together, Jessup."

"All right, Morgan . . . what's the big payoff?"

"A job with the *top* man in your organization . . . permanent and with all the benefits."

"What makes you think there is such a man or such a job?"

"Because you don't have the stock for taking over half of Idaho. That will take a big cattle or railroad operation." Morgan smiled. "As for the job, yours will do fine." He added, hastily, "or one just like it." Jessup found no humor in Morgan's latter comments but he obviously had come to Ketchum to deal.

"I can deliver on all of those things, Morgan, except possibly one. You said you wanted in when the Rocky Barr is wiped out. If the judge agrees to get out that will be the ransom. If he's out, there's no need to destroy it."

"Bullshit! Your people want land . . . not buildings. I want to see it burn."

"Why?"

"That's my business and it's going to stay that

way, Jessup. As to the ransom. . . your people can pay me a third of what it's worth to them to acquire it.''

"You deliver the girl to me today . . . here. I'll get back to you about Horn.''

"Uh uh. I ride back with you. I talk to the top man with you. If everything is like you tell me it is, Mason here will deliver the girl. We can pick a spot later and I'll get word back to him. When the exchange is made I'll go after Horn.''

"I told you, Morgan . . . you're as high as you go . . . for now.''

"You told me that when we started this, Jessup. Now we're finished. Take it or leave it.''

"I told you, Morgan . . . don't push me.''

"And I'm telling you Jessup . . . we do it that way or I'll take what I can get for Morgana Barr and ride out.''

"You're a smarter man than I gave you credit for," Jessup said, smiling. "All right, Morgan, we'll do it your way.'' He turned to his men. "Get the horses and get ready to ride out. Zeke . . . you stay here with Mister Morgan and our hostess. If things don't go well you know what to do.'' He turned and smiled at Morgan. "My insurance . . . Mister Morgan.''

8

Lee Morgan was on the inside. The young, steely-eyed gunman found himself the object of considerable attention as he and Harv Jessup rode into the very bowels of Gunsmoke Gorge. Plenty of money had been spent to establish the base camp. Mogan could only guess of course, but he estimated facilities for about a hundred men.

Futher, Morgan figured it was about five miles from the entrance, well hidden and well guarded, to the lone, wooden building in the camp.

"All the comforts," Morgan observed as he and Jessup dismounted. "At least for the ramrods." It was cold. Morgan glanced back at the rows of tents pitched on either side of the rocky gorge. They housed the riders.

"They're all equipped with coal oil stoves," Jessup said. "Besides, it's perfectly safe to build fires down in here." He pointed to the sheer rock walls on either side. "There's a constant wind at the top. Flattens the smoke out and disperses it before it ever carries too high. You'd have to be within a mile to see it." He grinned. "Even then, Morgan, what the hell good would it do you?"

"None," Morgan said, "from what I could see when we were riding in. I'm impressed."

He was even more impressed inside the two room

shack. The raiders were listed in varying unit strengths with military precision. On the wall, behind the only desk, a topographical map indicated Idaho ranches. Marked in red were those which had been destroyed. Green indicated those still in operation. Yellow marked ranches which had simply been abandoned by frightened families.

Morgan turned to his left at the sound of footsteps. Emerging from the small bedroom was a tall, distinguished looking, well dressed man. he was attired in a suit but Morgan could see the telltale bulge of a shoulder holster.

"This is Lee Morgan," Jessup said. "He wants in. He looks and sounds as though he'd fit and he's got a head start on contributing to our cause."

The man nodded at Jessup and gave Morgan a studied going over.

"I'm Brock," he said. "That's name enough." He moved over behind the desk. "A drink, Mister Morgan?"

"Yeah . . . fine."

Brock poured three. Morgan noted the small quantity. "Welcome," Brock said. They all drank. Brock nodded for Jessup and Morgan to sit. They did. "One of Harv's men rode in late last night. He told me what you've done. . . who you've got and what you want. I know something of your background, Mister Morgan, so I'll ask the question. *Why?*"

"Because Judge Isaac Barr was responsible for my father's death," Morgan lied. "Indirectly, anyhow."

"I'm not in this to aid men in carrying out personal vendettas, Mister Morgan. There is too much at stake."

"I know what's at stake . . . at least enough to

know I want in.'' Morgan was cool, relaxed and felt on sure footing. ''Old man Barr is just a bonus I'll get out of it.''

''Your demands are . . . shall we say . . . quite ambitious.''

''Yeah . . . but what I can deliver is more than you've been able to accomplish. Eventually, the army will get dragged into this unless you do the job quick and clean. I don't think even what you've got here is adequate if that happens.''

''Of course, sir, you are correct. That's why you've been permitted to live this long.'' Brock leaned back and put his fingertips together. ''But make no mistake, Mister Morgan, you'll be expected to deliver your end, in full, before I'm convinced.''

''I don't have a problem with that Brock . . . just with bastards that try to double-cross me.''

''Yes. . . I can appreciate that and, frankly, I don't understand what happened to Mister Lambert. If, in fact, he did try such a thing, you only did what I would have had to order done anyway. You see if we allow that kind of thing, we'll soon have no trust from those men outside. It is them upon whom we rely to get the job done.''

''You doubting my word about Lambert?''

''It's academic isn't it? He's certainly in no position to defend himself against your accusations. Let's just say that I'll be both happy and convinced if you can deliver on your claims. If not, I'll have you killed, Mister Morgan. It's really just that simple.''

''And if I *do* deliver?''

''Your demands . . . or shall we call them requests . . . will be met. No questions asked.''

''What's your reaction to Morgan's claim about Tom Horn?'' Jessup asked. He looked at Morgan as he posed the question.

"Someone is out there. We've already taken losses," Brock said. "One man . . . particularly one with Horn's reputation, can be more damaging to us than a cavalry company. He *must* be stopped." Brock leaned forward. "Whether or not it's Tom Horn really doesn't matter, does it, Jessup?"

"I guess not."

"Morgan," Brock said, getting to his feet, "you write up the necessary message to get the Barr woman up here. Once that's done, Tom Horn is all yours." Brock smiled. "Make certain you live to collect, Mister Morgan."

"If I don't, you're the winner again aren't you?"

"I'd say so. Not even Tom Horn can take all my men out. Now then, Jessup will arrange quarters for you."

"I want to see Strada's neice." Jessup's head jerked toward Morgan. Brock frowned. "I don't want Morgana Barr killed no matter what happens. If Strada's niece is actually up here . . . still alive . . . then I want to know it for certain."

"You have other plans for Miss Barr," Brock asked, grinning.

"Let's just say I want her breathing and leave it at that."

"You've got iron, Mister Morgan. A lot of iron. If you're what you seem, we'll get along just fine. Very well then, Jessup will take you to the girl. One more thing, Mister Morgan."

"Yeah?"

"There are two small ranches just this side of Killerman's place. Joe Galbraith and Todd Blaisdell. They've given us some trouble."

"What about it?'

"We're taking them out—in the morning," Brock

said, smiling. "I'd like you to lead one of the raiding parties. You can have your choice. It's just that everyone in the Gorge has to earn their keep. In your case . . . until you've done for us what you say you can . . . this will be, uh, a token gesture of good faith. Any problems with that, Mister Morgan?"

There were plenty and Morgan knew it but there wasn't a damned thing he could do about it. He didn't dare even hesitate. "None at all, Brock. I'll take the Blaisdell place. I met Galbraith once . . . a long time back but there's no use taking chances."

"Very good Mister Morgan . . . yes . . . very good indeed. The men will form up at dawn."

"I'll be ready."

Harv Jessup led Morgan to an isolated tent behind the house. Two men guarded it. "The girl's in there," Jessup said. Morgan nodded, ducked low and entered. Instantly, he put his index finger to his lips. The girl frowned. She was tied but not gagged. He knelt by her.

"You're about to have company," he said, loudly. "Morgana Barr. I imagine you know her . . . don't you?" The girl's eyes showed fear but she nodded.

Morgan leaned down and pulled her head close to him. "Don't make a sound," he whispered. "I'm here to get you out. It won't happen right away . . . but you'll be safe." He got up and looked into her face. Such a tactic was always risky. She blinked. He could see the moisture in her eyes. She nodded.

Morgan left the tent. Jessup was standing nearby talking to one of the guards. He turned. "You satisfied?" Morgan nodded. "Then let's get you bedded down. Sounds like you've got some riding to do in the morning." Morgan knew Jessup was particularly pleased that Brock had ordered the rails and collared Morgan to lead one of them. As for Lee

. . . he didn't know what the hell he was going to do.

Tom Horn, by contrast, knew exactly what he was going to do. He found a cutaway in a craggy, rock wall and made camp. There was a light snow beginning to fall again but inside the cutaway, he could build a fire. It also provided a good vantage point from which to view the valley below. Just half an hour earlier, he'd spotted a lone rider headed west. He assumed it to be one of the raiders and decided to gamble that, eventually, the man would return. At that point, Tom would trail him to Gunsmoke Gorge. In fact, the man Horn had seen was the messenger riding out to fetch back Judge Barr's daughter.

During the three days that Morgan had cooled his heels in Ketchum, Horn had followed several trails. Thus far, all of them had been dead ends.

After his encounter with his would-be killers, Horn doubled back to the Killerman ranch. There, he spent the night and learned that Ben Strada had not been at the ranch. It puzzled him, given the trail he followed which he believed was Strada's. Killerman himself was none too receptive to Horn. He'd voted against Horn's hiring. Josh Killerman was a man who believed negotiation was the best settlement of dispute.

On the second day out, Tom had hoped to pick up Strada's trail again but a new snowfall stifled the effort. Instead, he stopped by several small ranches and visited with their owners. He did his best to bolster their spirits. Most of them had heard about Strada's niece and they were certain Strada would knuckle under. If he went Killerman would follow. Soon, the small ranch owners would be on their own. That, Horn knew, would finish them.

He spent most of the third day swinging far to the southeast. If he was going to approach the Gunsmoke Gorge area again, it would have to be from a direction much less obvious than the one he tried earlier. His trail brought him to the rocky cutaway and his present campsite.

Dawn brought a familiar sound to Tom Horn's ears. The rumble of distant hoofbeats . . . a lot of them. He grabbed the Creedmoor and moved outside the cutaway.

"Movin' out fer a raid," he said to himself, aloud. He counted more than thirty riders. They were following about the same trail that the lone rider he'd seen the day before taking. "Well, sir . . . they hired me. Guess I'd best earn my keep." He hurried back to the cave and picked up both his Winchester and the Henry he'd taken from one of his two assailants. He dug into his gear and produced two boxes of ammunition.

By the time he got back to his vantage point, the lead riders were almost parallel with him. He'd wait a moment more. The Creedmoor would furnish his introduction. He figured he could take at least two men out before the riders would react. After that, he'd use the repeaters and go after some of the mounts. As for himself, he was in the best possible position. Completely out of reach of his enemies. The only way up was the way he'd come and those riders were nearly three miles away from the trail.

He line sighted the fifth man from the end and fired. The Creedmoor sounded like a Napoleon gun among the rocks. The man dropped. Two riders behind him pulled up short. He slammed another .44-90 into the chamber and fired again. Another man dropped. He hefted the Henry.

"Where the fuck is he?" one of the men screamed. Several dismounted and found the best cover they could. The lead riders turned and stopped. Even at horses, the distance provided a real challenge for a marksman. Tom Horn met the challenge. One . . . two . . . three mounts went down. One man was struggling to get to his feet. Horn went back to the Creedmoor.

A man named Lyle Buford had been picked to lead the second raid. He was riding up front with Morgan. Morgan knew almost at once that Tom Horn was doing his job. He finally turned to Buford.

"That son-of-a-bitch will take out a dozen men if we don't stop him. That's what I'm here for and I'm not missing the chance. Get the men back to camp. We'll have to hit the ranches another time. I'm going after Horn."

"That ain't part o' the orders."

"Those are my orders," Morgan said, spurring Pacer and shouting back as he rode off. "Do as you goddam please, Buford, but that son-of-a-bitch will kill you if you stay where you are."

Harv Jessup ran half the length of the camp to be first at Brock's cabin. Brock was just sitting down with a cup of coffee.

"The men are back . . . that is . . . some of 'em." Brock looked up, quizzically. "Somethin's wrong."

"Morgan?"

"Don't know. So far . . . all I've seen is Lyle. He's ridin' up now."

Buford told the men what had happened. All totalled, Tom Horn had taken out four men and seven animals. Only the men's retreat had kept him from a higher toll.

"And you say Morgan ⸗claimed it was Tom

Horn?''

"That's what he said . . . and that he was goin'
after him." Brock assumed a studied expression.
Finally, he shook his head.

"He couldn't have known," Brock said. "I didn't
really plan those raids until he got here."

"And I had a man ridin' drag—trailed us all the
way from Ketchum," Jessup said. "Nobody
followed *us*."

Brock got to his feet. "Lyle . . . you were out there.
What do you think?"

Buford smiled. "I think Mogan's all right," he
answered, "but I put Joe Banks on him anyways.
Banks is about the best tracker we got. Morgan
won't lose 'im and Banks can handle himself if
there's trouble."

"Good thinking," Brock said. "Now . . . with
Morgan preoccupied and Horn . . . or whoever it was
that shot us up . . . figuring he stopped us, we'll try
it again. Harv . . . you lead it. Take thirty men and
hit those ranches . . . hit them hard. We don't want
any of them getting the idea that there's hope riding
around out there."

Lee Morgan hadn't been in the Bitterroot country
for some time but he knew that the man who'd shot
up the raiders could only be in one or two spots. He
picked the right one on the first try. Half way up the
trail to where Horn was located, Morgan knew he
was being trailed. He opted for the easy way out.

He dismounted, let Pacer have his head, up trail,
slipped into the confines of some nearby trees and
waited. A few minutes later, a rider came into view.
Morgan smiled, pointed the Winchester into the air
and fired twice.

The rider, Joe Banks, reacted predictably. Since

neither shot came anywhere near him, he assumed Morgan had found a target . . . or someone was using Morgan for a target. There was a bend in the trail about fifty yards beyond Morgan's hiding place. Banks spurred his mount and rode past Morgan at a gallop. He reached the bend, reined up and dismounted. Morgan came out of the trees, raised the Winchester and waited. If he was right . . . if Tom Horn was up trail, Morgan would know it in a moment. If not he'd take Banks out.

The Creedmoor's roar answered Morgan's question. Joe Banks died instantly. When the shot's echo died away, Morgan hollered.

"Horn . . . it's Lee Morgan." There was no reply. A moment later, Morgan heard a noise above and slightly behind him. He crouched and spun around, looking up. Tom Horn was smiling down . . . Creedmoor at the ready. "You're one up on me," Morgan said.

"Well," Horn replied with his slow drawl, "that's just about right. I don't much like bein' even up with a man . . . an' I plumb hate losin'." Horn motioned off to his right. "Camp's back up there, ride in."

Horn and Morgan rounded up Banks' horse, wrapped Banks' body in his own bedroll and then sat down and exchanged information. Horn talked first. He was just finishing up by expressing his puzzlement about Ben Strada when the two men heard the riders. They moved to Horn's lookout position.

"Shit," Morgan exclaimed. "They're moving right out again . . . going after the Galbraith place and the Blaisdell spread."

"That where you were headed?" Morgan nodded. "Well . . . they can burn 'em out but they won't find

no people. Ever'body's meetin' at Killerman's ranch
today. S'posed to be gettin' some word down from
the Guv'nor's office." They watched the riders until
they were out of sight. They returned to Horn's
camp and Morgan then told his story. He got a
distinct reaction from Tom Horn when, toward the
conclusion of his story, he mentioned Brock's name.

"This fella Brock . . . what's he look like?"

"Tall . . . clean shaven . . . graying a little. Dresses
nice. Wears a shoulder rig."

"Got a little twitch in his left eye?" Morgan
looked up. He was clearly surprised.

"Yeah Tom . . . matter of fact, he does."

"I'll be damned. That there would be Riley
Brock."

"You know 'im?"

"Did once'st. Rode a posse with 'im . . . down in
Texas. We was lookin' for Big Ben Kilcannon an' his
cattle thievin' bunch."

"Brock was a lawman?"

"Pinkerton agent . . . one o' the best. Faster'n hell
an' got a head fer figgerin' things out." Horn shoved
his hat back on his head, rubbed the end of his nose
and then continued. "Dedicated too. Too young fer
the war but figgered ever' man owed his country. He
was doin' his time in *gummint* service by workin' fer
the President."

"You sound surprised that he'd go bad."

"I am. Not that kind o' man. I ain't sayin' he's not
givin' the orders down there, Morgan . . . but if'n he
is my guess would be that he's workin' fer somebody
bigger. Railroad mebbe . . . but somebody he
respects. He was a mighty set fella . . . always figgered that whatever was best fer the country was
the best thing to do . . . no matter how many little
fellas got hurt along the way."

"Then what you're saying doesn't make him the top man . . . if you're right."

"I'd wager on it. He might be the ramrod out there, but they's bigger fish he's answerin' to."

"That's an edge that'll come in damned handy," Morgan said. "I think he trusts me more than not."

"How you figgerin' to explain that," Horn asked, pointing to Banks' body, "an' not gettin' me?"

Morgan grinned. "I've been pondering that Tom. Banks can take the blame. He won't complain about it." Horn snickered. "You mind giving up the Creedmoor?" Horn frowned. "It may convince Brock that I was close . . . damned close. Close enough you had to ride out kinda sudden like. The Creedmoor isn't something you'd likely give up easy. I'll just tell him I'd have had you except Banks there got in the road."

Horn got to his feet. "You're the only son-of-a-bitch I ever rode with what could get that piece without killin' me fer it."

"It's the only way I'd want to try," Morgan said.

"Well . . . since you're on the inside and I know what I need to know . . . think I'll ride on back to Killerman's place . . . see how their meetin' went. I'll do some snoopin'," Horn continued, "smell out what I can about Brock."

"We need a way to get word back and forth to each other," Morgan said. "There's an abandoned mine shack about fifteen miles from here . . . southwest. Follow Leadore creek where it angles off toward Flintiron Mountain."

"That's the big 'un ain't it?"

"Yeah. The shack's easy to spot. Almost at the base of the mountain. Anything important . . . leave it there. Let's try to meet there in a week." Horn nodded and the two men shook hands. Horn waited until Morgan was back down in the valley and then he packed his gear and broke camp. He was almost ready to ride out when he heard hoofbeats again. He checked. The marauders were returning from their raids. They were riding hard and he figured they'd overtake Morgan before he got back to Gunsmoke Gorge.

"Watch yourself, boy," he said, aloud. As he turned to head back to his animals, he spotted two more riders. Just behind them, rode gun drummer Mason and Morgana Barr. "Things is shapin' up in a hurry," he mumbled.

9

Morgan too had heard the returning riders coming up on him. He broke his trail and stayed out of sight. Similarly, he spotted men bringing in Morgana Barr. He decided to stay out until nightfall. It was risky but he was betting that whoever was standing guard would let him through when they saw Banks' body. He was right. He rode up to Brock's shack just before midnight.

"You're a puzzlement to me," Brock said, "a disturbing one. I don't like to be disturbed, Morgan."

"Barr's daughter is here like I said. You lost men to Tom Horn. Like I said and you burned out a couple of insignificant ranches without accomplishing a damned thing. Frankly," Morgan said, leaning back against the wall and folding his arms, "it's *me* that ought to be *disturbed*. I had Horn dead to rights and your man Banks fucked it up."

"All I've got is your word." Morgan turned suddenly, exited the shack and returned a moment later with the Creedmoor. He tossed it to Brock— hard. Its weight stung Brock's hands when he caught it. He winced. He looked down at it.

"You think Horn would give *that* up. I was that close Brock . . . close enough to force him out. Banks goddam near got us both killed. That won't happen again, Mister Brock."

"You telling me this is Tom Horn's Creedmoor?"

"I don't have to tell you that, Brock," Morgan said, scathingly. "Look at the goddam initials on it . . . and the date. Before the Creedmoor I heard that Horn used to use a .50 caliber Sharps. That right?"

"How the hell would I know?"

"Because you rode posse with him . . . once anyway . . . down in Texas, wasn't it?" Morgan's cool headed use of the information he possessed now payed handsome dividends. Brock visibly displayed his surprise.

"You figure me a two bit gunny with a greedy heart and Harv Jessup's mind . . . or maybe Lambert's . . . or Banks' out there. I'm not and the sooner you believe that, the better chance you got of stayin' alive." Morgan had played out the whole hand . . . at least all the cards he held at the present time. He leaned back again smiling.

Brock considered him. He stood the Creedmoor in the corner and then sat down at his desk. "You're clever all right," Brock finally said. "That's the part that bothers me most. Maybe you're just clever enough to pull off what nobody else could."

"That the Pinkerton in you Brock?"

"Seems you've got all the answers, Morgan."

"Not quite."

"Really? What's missing?"

"The top man," Morgan replied. He straightened, walked to Brock's desk, rested his weight on his hands and leaned down . . . close to Brock's face. "Who do you work for," he asked.

"Morgan . . . you're pushing too hard . . . too fast."

"Then you're not denying there *is* somebody higher."

"I'm not denying . . or *confirming* a damned thing for you."

"Have it your way, Brock," Morgan said, smiling. "The one thing I've got that you don't is time . . . plenty of time." He straightened, walked over and picked up the Creedmoor, walked to the door, turned back and flicked the brim of his hat in a somewhat contemptuous gesture of goodbye and walked out.

Morgan stashed the rifle with his gear and then went over to the tent where Strada's niece was being held. The guards showed signs of wanting to stop him but his steely-eyed stares backed them down. He went in and found, as he'd expected, Morgana Barr. Again, he gestured for silence. He waited, quietly, for a moment and then stepped back outside.

"You boys go for a little walk." He was grinning. "Half of that in there," he said, smiling, "is my property. I am to do a little inspecting." The two men looked at each other and finally one of them shrugged. They walked off to some nearby trees and rolled themselves some smokes.

"You can talk now," Morgan said, "if you keep it low."

"I didn't think you would let it go this far," Morgana said. Her tone belied her calm appearance.

"You'll be safe. Don't worry." He turned to Strada's niece. "Your name?"

"Lileth Joy Johnson," she said. "My mother is Ben Strada's sister."

Morgan nodded. "Sorry . . . but I didn't remember the name . . . Lileth. What do folks call you?"

"Lil . . . mostly."

Morgan recalled that she was twenty-five. She looked older. She had long copper hair. Her face was small . . . mostly like the rest of her . . . except, Morgan noted, her breasts. She was only about five feet, two inches tall but she had large, pendulous breasts. His eyeing of them did not go unnoticed by either woman.

"We're going to get you both out of here," Morgan said, "and safely. You'll just have to be patient until I can make my move."

"My uncle may have me out before that," the girl said. Her tone was somewhat disrespectful of Morgan's claim. "He knows the right people . . . the people to talk to . . . the people who will take action at once."

"If you mean the Governor," Morgan said, "forget it." Morgan turned to her. "What do you mean?"

"My father helped to elect that man . . . if the Governor is obligated to anyone . . . it's my father. He turned my father down. I fail to see how this . . . this girl's uncle is going to help."

"Your father is not the man he once was," Lil said. "Ben Strada gets things done in Idaho today with action—not on a worn out reputation." Morgana Barr jerked toward the girl. She couldn't reach her. Morgan slipped between them.

"You keep this up and you'll get us all killed. Get along," he said. He got up. "After it's over . . . you can scratch each other's eyes out . . . I don't give a damn. For now . . . get along."

Morgan lay in his tent wide awake. He had mixed emotions. He was glad both women were safe but he was troubled by their petty jealousy and concerned about Ben Strada. Horn suspected Strada could be on the wrong side in the fight and yet Strada's niece was certain he'd use all his power to negotiate her release. Strada might have more answers to questions than Morgan realized. He decided that finding Strada was his next move.

The new day brought the news that Brock had

ordered another raid. This time on the Elk Horn Ranch about twenty miles due south. The marauders struck paydirt there. The ranch's owner, Silas Freeborn, was killed. So were ten ranch hands and Freeborn's brother. All the buildings were burned out. By Brock's accounting, it was a complete success.

"One more down," he said, marking the big wall map. He turned back to Morgan, whom he'd summoned just after sunup. "I was kept up most of the night," he said smiling. He seemed to Morgan . . . almost congenial. "I was thinking about you. You're a good man, Morgan, a good man to have on my side. I'm through doubting. You're in. No more raids, no more . . . well, *proof.* Get me Tom Horn. In the meantime, I'll begin contacts to negotiate with Strada and Judge Barr. You'll be well taken care of. You have my word on it."

Morgan was wary but now it was Brock who was holding cards and he proved himself a worthy player. Enticing Morgan with things that, right now, Morgan couldn't prove one way or the other. He had to play along. "When the time comes . . . soon it will be too . . . you'll meet the *right* people. I promise you that, Morgan." He walked up and offered his hand. "Deal?"

Morgan continued to study Brock's eyes for a few moments. The information had come fast. Brock had all but admitted that there were higher-ups. If the land war in Idaho was ever to be ended, it was these men . . . these right people to whom Brock alluded, that would have to be brought down.

"Deal," Morgan finally said. They shook hands. "I saw the women last night. I want . . . uh, some time with them before they're turned back to their relatives." Morgan grinned.

"Fine," Brock said. He wasn't grinning. Lee was about to learn that Brock's icy exterior was not just a facade. "You can have them first. A few of the other men have earned some rewards as well. Oh . . . by the way," Brock said, reaching beneath his desk, "you might want this. After all . . . to the victor as they say." He handed Morgan the guncase which had belonged to Mason. Morgan frowned.

"I know he was your man but he was an outsider. Besides, you've got run of camp and anything else you need now. I didn't figure you'd care."

"Care? About *what?*"

"Why Mason, of course. I had him shot."

Tom Horn rode into the middle of one hell of a fight. It was the worst possible kind . . . at least as far as Tom was concerned. Neighbor fighting neighbor . . . or arguing loudly, at least. The ranchers were split about down the middle over the latest incidents. One of those incidents shocked even Tom Horn.

Tom knew that Josh Killerman didn't have a lot of use for him but the expression on Killerman's face when he answered Tom's knock at the door was one of hatred.

"You're a nervy son-of-a-bitch," Killerman said. "I'll give you that much." He grabbed Tom's coat collars and pulled him inside. The aging manhunter tried to defend himself but two more men jumped him. He took some hard blows to the solar plexis and finally to the jaw. He went down. Someone kicked him.

"That's enough!"

"Not near enough, Marshal."

"Don't make me draw a gun in your house Josh . . . now damn it, back off." The men moved back and Marshal Seth Rawlings got Tom Horn back on his feet.

"You plannin' on takin' him out o' here, Marshal?" Rawlings didn't like the question. He scowled at the man who'd asked it. He moved Tom to the dining room and sat him down in a chair.

"Now," he said, turning to the men . . . about a dozen of them, "I want to hear what Mister Horn has to say. If I don't like it or I don't believe it or it can't be verified, then he goes back to Boise with me. Anybody tries to make it different is bustin' the same law."

"He's a murderin' bastard, Marshal. You already know that. You don't need no evidence . . . and neither do we . . . none we ain't already got."

"I'm warning you, Parsons. I'll kill any man interfering with my job." The men present were obviously angry to the point of revenge. One of them, Tom noted, had a rope. Nonetheless, they knew Seth Rawlings and, for the time being at least, backed off.

"Horn," the marshal said, looking into Tom's face. "Ben Strada is dead. Shot from ambush. Most here figure you did it. Whether by mistake or design they don't know. Right now they don't care."

"Seems to me you don't much care either, Marshal."

"I got a job, Horn. I'll do it. Like it or not."

"I didn't shoot Strada. Ain't seen 'im."

"You killed his man," Rawlings said, "Toby Summers. Lyin' about it won't help you none either. Found Summers blowed apart by a heavy caliber rifle . . . no scatter gun. You carry a Creedmoor don't you?"

Tom looked into Rawlings' eyes and then around the room. He half smiled. "I killed Summers right

enough 'cause if I hadn't, he'd uh killed me. An'
yeah . . . I got me a Creedmoor, or I did anyways.''

"You *did?*"

"I lost it durin' a run-in with some marauders.
Anyways . . . I didn't kill Strada."

"But you admit killing Summers?" Horn nodded.
"They were together."

"They weren't the last time I saw 'em."

"You just told us you hadn't seen Ben Strada."

"Marshal, I can tell you a whole heap o' things,
but this ain't the time," he looked around again,
"an' it sure as hell ain't the place."

"I'll decide that," Rawlings shot back, "not you.
Anything you got to say, you say it here and now.
I'll stick by you because it's my job, but these
people deserve to know the truth."

"We won't be gettin' any o' that from Tom Horn.
He's a lyin', payed for killin' bastard. Ben was shot
with the same gun what killed Summers . . . an' the
rest o' them at the shack too."

"An' two men that tried to bushwhack me later
and four o' the raiders and a half a dozen o' their
mounts," Horn said. "I had my suspects about
Strada but I didn't kill 'em. I been up in the Bitterroots for near a week."

Rawlings frowned. "Where was Strada killed?"

"Between Boise and the Rocky Barr ranch. Found
him down along the Middle Fork after we tracked
his mount back. The horse was one he'd taken from
Judge Barr's place. He just went on home."

"Horn said he was out a week . . . been all o' that
an' more. He had plenty o' time to get Ben."

"But I didn't . . . an' how you know he was done in
with a Creedmoor?"

"Because the bullet was still in him," Rawlings
said. "He was shot from one helluva distance. It's

not the kind of a shot many men can make. At least
. . . none from around here."

Tom Horn grinned. "There must be two hunnert
gunmen in this valley right now . . . on both sides o'
the law. Out o' that many . . . a few are good. Hell
fire . . . Toby Summers could o' made a shot like
that."

"I told you Horn . . . if I didn't like your answers
or I didn't believe you . . . we'd head for Boise."

Rawlings stepped back, drew his pistol and said,
"Let's go."

Tom stood up. "Which is it, Marshal? You don't
believe me or you just don't like what you hear?"

"No matter . . . we're goin' to Boise either way."

"He done it, Marshal an' he's gonna pay for it."
One of the men bulled their way through the others
but Rawlings whirled and caught the man on the
jaw with the barrel of the Colt's. He and Tom then
backed out of the ranch house to their horses.

"It's a long way to Boise," one man yelled.

"You'd best keep these men in line, Josh,"
Rawlings warned.

"You did your job, Marshal . . . none of 'em would
be here."

"And if your association didn't hire on mankillers
. . . I'd be out tryin' to do that job." The marshal
mounted and then turned to Tom. "I want your
word you'll ride with me clean."

"You got it," Tom said. "Time we get to Boise . . .
you'll be thinkin' differ'nt."

Lee Morgan had planned to ride out of the Gorge
that very day. The news about Mason and Brock's
change of mind . . . if not heart . . . held him back.
Now, he figured, he'd have a chance at finding out
when and where Brock planned his next raid.

Perhaps he could warn the would-be victims or, at worst, somehow foil the attempt.

On the pretext of giving Tom Horn a day or two in which to re-position himself, Morgan payed Brock a visit that evening. Brock was out of the shack. Morgan was tempted to try a quick search but he considered the risk too great. He was firmly ensconced with Brock now and whatever he might find in the shack would be of little value if he got caught.

He simply took a bottle of whiskey off a shelf, opened it and sat down at Brock's desk to wait. When he started to pour himself a second drink, he noticed a single name, hastily scratched on a piece of paper. *Belle*. Belle Moran? Boise? He wondered. Why would Brock have jotted down so unlikely as name as hers? The door opened.

"Well now," Brock said, "I rather hoped you'd be out hunting Tom Horn." The door closed. Morgan twisted around and hefted his glass in a gesture of greeting.

"Horn will need a day or two to find another roosting place. There are one or two likely spots. Tomorrow, I'll start checking them out."

Brock moved to the other side of the desk. Morgan noted that he made a hasty check of its order. He would have noticed almost anything that was out of place. There was nothing to notice.

"I've sent a rider to the Rocky Barr. I've decided to put some double pressure on the good judge. I informed him we had both his daughter and Strada's niece. I'll let him worry about handling that end."

"You planning to strengthen your position a little more?" Morgan sipped the whiskey and smiled, displaying an off-handed attitude.

"You mean another raid in conjunction with the notes?"

"Yeah . . . mebbe."

"Is that what you'd do?"

"Prob'ly. I'd like the judge to know we're still out here—that nothing's changed."

"We are Morgan . . . and it hasn't. As a matter of fact, I have something very close to that in mind." Brock smiled. "A little more ambitious perhaps . . . but similar. I'll be riding out myself tomorrow. Gone a week or more. When I get back I should have an answer from the judge. No matter what it is we're going to bring the rest of the ranchers in line once and for all."

"Sounds impressive," Morgan said. He felt a tension. Something big was in the making. He looked at Brock . . . hoping.

"Now what can I do for you?" Morgan realized that Brock would say no more. He didn't care to push the issue. He smiled, put the bottle on Brock's desk and got to his feet.

"You just did it, Brock. Thanks for the whiskey." Brock smiled.

10

The snow was wet and heavy and getting worse. The ride from the Rocking K had taken its toll on men and mounts. Seth Rawlings wanted no more.

"We're gonna hole up in Ketchum," he said. Tom Horn just nodded. The two men had hardly spoken a word since they left the Killerman spread. It was a long trip to Boise and Tom figured he'd have plenty of time to tell his tale.

Rawlings knew exactly where he wanted to go and it wasn't to any of the saloons. The last thing he needed was trouble. He rode straight to the parsonage. A few minutes later, he and Tom Horn were warming themselves by a cozy fire.

Ephram Culpepper walked in. He eyed both men and grinned. "Who's got who?" he asked.

"Howdy, Ephram," Rawlings said. They shook hands. Rawlings did a half turn. "This is Tom Horn."

"Yeah . . . I had that much figured out. Howdy, Mister Horn. I'm Culpepper . . . God's man in these here parts." Tom moved toward him, smiled and shook his hand.

"I've heard about you. Like what I heard too. Always kinda figured the Lord needed a hand in this country. Man like you gives Him a strong one."

"Some wouldn't agree."

"Some wouldn't agree with anythin'," Horn said. He glanced at the marshal. "By the way . . . he's takin' me in . . . to Boise."

"For *what*? I heard the ranchers hired you, Horn."

"You heard right," Seth Rawlings said, scowling. "A damned bad idea. Now . . . seems like Ben Strada's been shot . . . from ambush. Ranchers think Horn here did it . . . by accident maybe . . . but did it, just the same."

"What do you think, Seth?"

"I think the judge'll decide."

"How long you been out lookin'," Culpepper asked the marshal.

"Not long. I was up at the Rocky Barr when I heard. I got a message to ride over to Josh Killerman's place and I did. Horn here," Rawlings continued, gesturing, "rode in as big as you please."

"Not too smart for a guilty man is it?"

"Mebbe not . . . then again . . . mebbe it's the smartest thing a guilty man could do."

Culpepper's woman brought coffee and fresh baked pie. The three men ate and chatted about nothing in particular. Rawlings finished first. "Horn, I'd like to hear your side of the story. All of it."

"Me too," Culpepper said, grinning. "Then, Marshal, you can mosey on over to Addie's place and arrest the man who *did* gun down Ben Strada." Both Rawlings and Horn were shocked. Culpepper, still grinning, just nodded. "Been holed up there for three days . . . roarin' drunk, braggin' about it. Says nobody will do anythin' since he's workin' for the *right* people."

Marshal Seth Rawlings listened closely, eyed Culpepper with considerable suspicion and then

said, "How's come you didn't go take 'im out
Ephram? I was given to understand you, more or
less, keep the law in Ketchum. Particularly where
Addie is involved."

"Real easy answer, Seth. They's five more of 'em
over there. Ever' one a gunny. Tried to weasel in on
Idaho's troubles. Seems neither side wanted 'em,
but from what I can gather, Ben Strada run 'em
clean off 'n his spread. Fella what shot Ben
didn't take kindly to that an' he's got a long
memory."

"You speak like you know 'im," Tom said.

"I do. So do you an' the marshal here too. Jess
Blanchard."

"Shit!"

"Yeah . . . an' his two brothers."

"You know the other two?"

"Only one of 'em. Sam Beecher. I figure it was big
Sam's gun what Jess used to kill Ben Strada."

"It was," Tom said. "And it is a Creedmoor .44-90
just like mine, or the one I had."

"Speakin' of that," Seth said, frowning, "you're
not a man that loses his gun. That made me itchier
than anythin' else you said."

"I didn't lose it. I gave it to young Lee Morgan.
He's on the inside now . . . ridin' with the marauders.
He had reason to want my gun. A damn good
reason. He's got it. He's got Morgana Barr too an'
by now, I'd wager, he knows the whereabouts of
Strada's niece."

"Why the hell didn't you tell me that back at
Killerman's place?"

"*You* know who you can trust out o' that bunch,
Marshal?" Tom Horn shook his head. "I damn well
don't, an' I didn't live this many years by gettin'
careless." Rawlings nodded. Tom Horn was right

and he knew it.

"Well, Marshal, what'll it be? Jess Blanchard gonna ride out?"

"He won't come in without a fight," Seth said, "an' you know it."

"I'll stand with you, Marshal. Two or three o' them fellas got prices on their hats . . ." Culpepper grinned, "Muh church here could use the money." Both he and Seth turned to Tom Horn.

"Seems about the only way I'll ever convince them fellas back at Killerman's place that I didn't do it."

"The odds aren't exactly on our side," Seth said. "Horn . . . you're not a gun hand . . . that is with a pistol."

Tom took his hat off, held it just above the top of his head and then scratched with his little finger. "Nope . . . but I'm pretty handy at evenin' up them odds you mentioned."

"You'll be wearing a badge, Horn . . . or you won't be going. When you got a star on you give a man a chance."

"Yep . . . I figgered on that, Marshal. I'll give 'em as much as I can . . . an' still keep breathin. That there is about the best offer I can make you."

"I'll get the badges," Seth said.

"I got me a brand new Remington shotgun," Culpepper said to Tom. "I'd be mighty proud if'n Tom Horn was the first man to use it."

"Obliged," Tom said, smiling. "I'll be glad to."

Marshal Seth Rawlings returned a few minutes later with two tin stars. He pinned one on each man's coat and then turned to face them.

"Raise your right hands," he said. They did. "You're swore," he said. "We'll go in an' get 'em at first light. Mebbe they'll be liquored up . . . or still asleep. For now . . . that's what I plan on doin' . . . gettin' some sleep.''

Marshal Rawlings, Tom Horn and Ephram Culpepper all came out of their beds in the small hours of the morning. A loud and persistent knocking had aroused them. They converged in the hallway just after Culpepper's woman had opened the door. The question as to whom was the most surprised remained unanswered. Four men stood staring at each other. Rawlings, Culpepper, Horn and Lee Morgan!

The clouds were gone . . . with them, that heavy, wet snow. The sky was the purplish-blue it becomes, just before full daylight on an icy morning. Lee Morgan's internal alarm clock brought him out of bed at 5:15. It was a quarter hour before he'd planned but Tom Horn's moving about had awakened him.

"I didn't git a chanc'st to ask you, Morgan," Tom Horn said, "but did you bring my rifle?"

"I did. You planning on using it today?"

"Not likely. The Winchester prob'ly."

"And Culpepper's new scatter-gun."

"Yeah . . . that too."

Lee had ridden hard, even with the deep, high country snow, to reach Ketchum by the night before. He could still scarcely believe the dumb luck of running into Tom Horn and the marshal. He'd ridden from Gunsmoke Gorge with only two goals in mind. Find Horn and give him its location and then find Ben Strada. He intended to solicit Culpepper's aid. He had already achieved all his goals—and then some. Now, he pondered the price he might have to pay for them.

"Seth pin a tin star on your coat yet?" Horn

asked, grinning.

"No . . . but he will, Tom."

"You mind?"

"I mind . . . but less than I used to. Anyway, for this job it seems right."

Tom Horn smiled and nodded. "The damned things always seem right when you're behind one."

Morgan pulled on his boots and stood up, stuffing in his shirt tail.

"Maybe . . . but I don't plan on making it permanent." The door opened and Ephram Culpepper stuck his head around it.

"Mornin' gents. The marshal says he's ready. Says to tell you *he'll* ask 'em to give it up . . . then he'll wait."

"An' if one of us gets shot he'll have his answer." Morgan strapped on his rig. Tom Horn smirked. They went downstairs.

"Horn . . . cover the back way out over at Addie's. Anybody comes through here is yours."

"Do *I* have to ask 'em anything, Marshal?" Tom was grinning.

"No, Horn, you goddam well don't, and I don't like it that way." Seth Rawlings wasn't grinning.

The four men stepped into the morning air. Each took a short gasp as the cold invaded their lungs. Breath exhaled in steamy clouds, quickly enveloped whiskers and froze in place. Only Lee Morgan was exempt.

The quartet of men reached the corner, moved to the middle of the street, their boots squeaking in the virgin snow. At the end of that street, they paused. Half a block away was Addie Terhune's place. A ribbon of white smoke curled up from the roof, itself appearing amost frozen in place. Seth Rawlings reached out and slapped Tom Horn on the shoulder,

Horn nodded, stuck one arm up and waved and
trudged off toward the back of the saloon.

The remaining three men started across the
street, diagonally. At the center of the main street,
Morgan stopped.

"Somebody rode out . . . recent." The others
looked at Morgan's finger, pointing to the ground. A
single set of hoof prints had marred the newly fallen
snow. "The prints were headed west."

"How recent you figure?" Rawlings asked.
Ephram knelt down and then dropped to all fours to
get a closer look. He studied two of the prints, stood
up and brushed himself off.

"Hard to say fer sure, Marshal. Always is in the
snow but I'd guess not more'n a couple o' hours.
Now new snow in them prints an' no sign o' much
bustin' at the edges. Horse made 'em after the snow
froze."

"Who in hell would ride outa here that early?"

"A man with a mission," Lee Morgan replied,
looking west.

"What are you thinkin', Morgan?"

"These boys aren't particular who they work for . .
. highest wage'll buy what they got to sell. Couldn't
sell it to Strada . . . so they killed him. I'm sure he
spoke for the association. They been layin' around
. . . lettin' the word out that they're available."

"An' Tom Horn took out a few o' that fella
Brock's riders?"

"Yeah, Marshal. That's what I'm thinking."

"Well let's see to it Brock don't get no more'n one
of 'em." Rawlings and Morgan both looked at Culpepper. The wily old gunman turned Bible thumper
was looking off to the west deep in thought.

"What's on your mind?" the marshal asked.
Culpepper didn't answer. "Ephram?" Culpepper's

head jerked around. He smiled weakly and shrugged.

The rifle shot tore into Seth Rawlings' right leg, just above the knee. He'd dropped his hat and stooped to pick it up. He'd moved a little faster than his would-be killer had figured. Had he not done so, the shot would have been through his temple. As it was, Seth howled and fell forward.

Both Morgan and Culpepper were blasting away in the direction of the shot, high up, probably on the roof of Addie's place. They found no target but the fusillade drove off the rifleman and gave them a chance to pull Marshal Rawlings to cover.

"Goddam it!"

"You're out of it, Seth. You leg's broke."

"I'll be damned if I am. Get me a rifle." Seth, wincing in pain, twisted his body so that he could see Lee Morgan working his way along the building fronts. "Morgan, damn you, get back here."

"Sorry, Seth," Ephram said, "but unless one o' those gunnys busts out an' runs this way . . . looks like you'll have to sit this one out."

"Ephram! Goddamn you, Ephram. Get me a rifle. You're a damn deputy . . . you do as I tell you. Ephram!"

Behind Addie's place, Tom Horn had heard the shot. He'd pushed himself into a doorway opposite the back stairs leading from Addie Terhune's room. Then, there was only the silence of the morning. A moment later, he heard the crunching of snow above him. In another second, a man came into view. He was carrying a rifle. He jumped from the roof to the stairway balcony, ran down the stairs, turned and saw Tom Horn. His mouth flew open. It would remain open, frozen in place. Horn let go with the shotgun.

Instantly, Tom moved out of the doorway, cut, catty-corner across the narrow alley way and pressed himself against the wall of the saloon. He slammed another shell into the shotgun. He eased himself along the wall toward the back door.

Out front, Morgan had reached the main entrance. The outside doors were closed but the bat wings were tied open. Morgan couldn't see a damned thing for the half inch of ice on the windows. He hugged the wall. Ephram Culpepper had crossed the street and slipped into a doorway. Morgan looked over, nodded and then pointed to a rocker which sat just a few feet away on the opposite side of the big window in the front of Addie's saloon. Culpepper nodded.

Ephram Culpepper pumped three rounds into the plate glass widow. The first two simply pierced it. The third spider-webbed the center of the glass and the cracks in it converged on its center. The window seemed to explode.

Morgan dashed from his position, swung himself around the solid backed rocker, lifted and leaped forward, through the opening where the window had been. Culpepper, himself changing positions, heard three shots. Two were pistol shots, the third a rifle. The latter struck the wood just above his head. Culpepper stopped, turned to his right, looked toward the roof and let go two more shots. There was a grunt, a man's body teetered on the roof's edge and then fell backward. Culpepper darted into another doorway and commenced reloading.

Inside the saloon, Lee Morgan was crouched behind the street-side end of the bar. The rocker had provided good cover although the second shot had pierced the pack, splintered the wood and sent a sliver of it into Morgan's left hand. He yanked it out, tearing the skin in the process. He cursed underneath his breath.

"Addie," Morgan shouted, "it's Lee Morgan. You okay?" No reply. "Addie!" No reply. Morgan reloaded the Smith and Wesson. Inside the heavy pocket of the skeepskin coat, Morgan had tucked the old Bisley Colt's. "Addie," he shouted, trying again. No answer. He heard the squeaking of a door hinge upstairs. He stayed in a crouch but scurried along to the opposite end of the bar.

"Your woman's right up here," a man's voice hollered. Morgan stayed put. He caught a glimpse of a shadow just to his right. He turned. He heard the door open. Two shots rang out. Both were from outside. Culpepper? Morgan thought so. He took advantage of the distraction and he took a chance. He moved three feet to his right, removed his hat and tossed it onto the end of the bar, just above where he'd been and then he stood up.

Morgan's hat flew from the bar. Morgan saw the gunman, Louie Blanchard, one of Jess Blanchard's brothers. Morgan shot him between the eyes. Instantly, he went down again, this time twisting so that he was on his back. A figure appeared at the street end of the bar, silhouetted against the outside light. Morgan fired, the figure fired, Ephram Culpepper, just coming through the window opening, fired.

The man's shot missed Morgan's head by little more than the width of a razor. Morgan's shot struck the figure in the groin. Culpepper's shot smashed into the man's back and severed his spine. Ephram grunted and went down, face first.

"Ephram," Morgan shouted.

"I'm hit!" A woman screamed. There was the sickening series of thuds and bumps as a body bounced down the stairs. Two shots smashed into

the wall above Morgan's position . . . holding him
down. A shotgun roared and there was silence.

The first man to die in the fight had been Willy
Keene. He was a twenty-two year old, pock-faced
gunny with a bloated view of his own worth. Tom
Horn had killed him out back. The man on the
roof, dead by two shots from Jake Culpepper's gun,
was Sam Beecher. Morgan's victim, inside the
saloon, was Louie Blanchard and the one he and Culpepper had shared, at the end of the bar, was Rick
Blanchard. Morgan sat up.

"How bad you hit?" he asked Ephram.

"I'll live.

"*Horn!*"

"Yep . . . I'm here. Took out a fella up on the
balcony."

"That's five," Morgan said. "There was only
supposed to be six and one rode out."

"Stay put," Horn shouted back. "Jess Blanchard
had another brother . . . a kid name o' Eustis. Was
either him or Jess what rode out . . . but they's one
of 'em still here . . . upstairs."

"You sure?"

"Yep. One o' the girls is laying at the bottom o'
the stairs. Looks like she's got a breathin' problem
. . . throat's been cut."

"Addie?"

"Nope."

"What makes you think there's still one up
there?"

"Showed himself at the window o' Addie's room.
Spotted him and I come through the back door . . .
took out the fella on the balcony. Man I saw didn't
have time to get that far."

Ephram Culpepper sat up. His right arm, high up
near his shoulder, was bleeding profusely. He

winced as he tried to move it. Upstairs, a door opened. Morgan stood up.

"I'm comin' out," a voice shouted. Morgan looked up. He could see a man . . . rather more a boy. He was holding a sawed-off shotgun in his right hand. The barrel was resting beneath Addie Terhune's chin. His left hand was around her waist and in it, he held an old Colt's Dragoon. "Anybody even breathes, her head comes off."

Addie was naked. Her arms were pulled behind her and obviously tied. Her mouth was bleeding, her eyes were big and round and her body was covered with goose bumps. Even under the circumstances, Morgan couldn't help but look at her breasts. They were big, round and jiggling with every movement. The brown ends were protruding, hardened by the chilly air. The dark patch between her legs was bigger than on most women Morgan had seen.

"You won't make it," Morgan said.

"I'll make it." The Dragoon barked. The shot was nowhere near Morgan. He didn't move. Still, he knew that Eustis Blanchard would kill Addie . . . probably out of panic more than desire. It was Jess then who had ridden out of Ketchum. Morgan was now certain he knew why.

Eustis and Addie reached the bottom of the stairs. Eustis pushed Addie in front of him and began backing, slowly, toward the front door. Again, he fired. A shot in Tom Horn's direction and another at Morgan. Neither was close. He dropped the Dragoon, reached behind him and felt for the doorknob. He found it, turned, pulled and moved forward. The icy air rushed in, Addie stiffened as it engulfed her nakedness. Eustis Blanchard tightened his grip on her waist and pulled hard. She backed. He stepped outside. His eyes got big, blinked and went closed. The shotgun clattered to the wooden sidewalk and Eustis Blanchard crumpled into a heap. Addie moaned and dropped to her knees. Marshal Rawlings, delicately balancing himself with his left hand on the door jam, stepped into view. He was holding his pistol by the barrel.

"We got one of 'em alive anyway," he said.

11

None of the others had seen or heard Tom Horn leave Addie's saloon . . . but leave he did. No one could be sure just what Jess Blanchard was up to or what he knew, but they couldn't risk letting him reach Gunsmoke Gorge.

He had a two to three hour head start but Tom Horn had dogged many a man with far more than that. Besides, Blanchard couldn't know he was being trailed. Horn pushed his horse hard through the snow. The trail was clean and clear and by noon, Tom had narrowed the lead to no more than a quarter of an hour.

He swung off the trail and moved into a stand of trees along a ridge. The going would be tougher but he reasoned that Blanchard would, at some point soon, stop to rest. He was right. Jess Blanchard was at the crest of a hillock and looking down on the inviting sight of smoke from a house.

It was the small ranch home of Jude Bailey and his family. Bailey had missed being wiped out on three different raids but he knew—as did Tom Horn —that it was only a matter of time. Now Blanchard could do the job almost by himself. Tom didn't intend to let that happen.

He tethered his mount by a tree, slipped the Creedmoor out of its case, assembled it, loaded and then strolled, casually, to the spot where Blanchard had stopped. He looked toward the cabin. Blanchard was half way there . . . Horn estimated about 590 yards . . . a third of a mile. There was no wind. Tom knelt in the snow, resting his right elbow on a tree stump.

A woman exited the cabin. A man stepped out behind her.

"Damn," Tom Horn said, aloud. Jess Blanchard reined up and slipped a rifle from the saddle scabbard. Tom lowered the Creedmoor's barrel brace into his left hand, wiggled his torso until the butt was tight against his shoulder. He sighted. Blanchard raised his own rifle. The woman, bent over, now straightened up. She was looking right at Jess Blanchard. She screamed but the sound never reached Tom's ears. It might have had it not been drowned out. He squeezed the trigger and the huge gun recoiled, its barrel jumping up and the stock slamming into Tom's shoulder pad. Jess Blanchard was still sighting in on his own target when the .44-90 slammed into his back. He flew from the horse as though pulled by a rope.

The Baileys could not seem to thank Tom Horn enough. He learned that Bailey's men . . . only four of them, had long since abandoned him. Horn warned them to pack up and ride to Ketchum until the trouble was over. Tom then went through Blanchard's gear. He found only one thing of interest . . . a letter with a Boise postmark.

Blanchard,
    If you and your men can't get on at Strada's place, ride, alone, to the shack marked on the enclosed map. You'll find work waiting. *Don't* under any circum-

stances try the RB. We have it. Your money will be at FQ.

                                        TY

Morgan was about the calmest man in Ketchum. He knew why Tom Horn had ridden out but the fact didn't impress Marshal Rawlings. Rawlings and Culpepper both got treatment for their wounds and Morgan spent a couple of hours with Addie Terhune. Those things done, Culpepper and Morgan brought young Eustis Blanchard to the marshal.

"Best I can figure, boy; you've done nothing too bad yet. Leastways . . . not here," Rawlings continued, "and *here* is where you are and all I'm interested in. Now what were you boys up to?"

"You can't scare me, Marshal," the boy said, his voice quivering.

"Good," Rawlings said calmly. "Then it won't scare you none to know you'll *hang* for what happened here."

The boy's eyes got big. "You just said . . . I didn't do nothin'."

"But you're all I've got." Rawlings eyed both Morgan and Culpepper. He could read in their faces that they knew what he was doing. "I think them fancy lawyers got a name for it . . . guilt by association. No jury'll give a tinker's damn whether you gunned somebody or not. They'll sentence you to hang . . . an' I'll see to it you do . . . unless you want to tell me what your brother is up to."

"I . . . I don't know." Rawlings smirked. "I *swear* to you, Marshal, I *don't* know. I mean . . . Jess, he was s'posed to have somethin' worked out . . . he . . . he got a letter from Boise. He didn't tell me nothin' . . . he never did . . . hardly."

"You mentioned a letter. From who?" Blanchard

shrugged. "Jess never mentioned anybody?"

"Just once . . . uh, he said he had contact with the *big* boss." Morgan frowned. "Brock?"

"He never mentioned no name . . . but, well, it couldn't o' been Brock. Now he was a fella we was s'posed to meet east o' here. But Jess knew that before he got the letter from Boise."

"Did you see that letter?" Morgan asked.

"Not to read it . . . but it come from Boise . . . that's sure. An' Jess, he was real happy about it."

"Because it came from the man he called the *big* boss . . . right?" Blanchard nodded.

"Take him over and lock him up," Rawlings said to Culpepper.

"Marshal," Eustis said, whining, "you gotta help me . . . you just gotta."

"Why? You tellin' me you wouldn't have killed Addie Terhune?"

"I was just usin' her to get out . . . that's all. I swear it." Rawlings just stared at the boy and Eustis was led away, tears in his eyes. Seth then turned and eyed Morgan.

"What's eatin' at you?"

"Boise . . . and maybe some answers."

"Then you believe that kid?"

"I saw a reference to Belle Moran's place in Boise . . . on Brock's desk over in the Gorge. That much of what Blanchard said ties in."

"So what do you plan to do about it?"

Morgan got to his feet. "Nothing . . . right now anyway. Things are moving too damned fast. There's a showdown coming . . . a big one. Right now . . . I'd best get those women out."

Seth looked quizzical. "Shit Morgan . . . *how?*"

"Brock is gone. Probably meeting Mister Big over in Boise. Told me he'd be gone a week . . . mebbe more. When he gets back it'll be too late to do anything."

"And now?"

"Nobody will question me if I tell them Brock sent me in to get the women. It's likely the only time I'll have a chance."

"And when he finds out what you've done?"

Morgan grinned. "He'll be mad as hell."

"What about Horn?"

"If he did what he went to do, Jess Blanchard is dead. Horn will be back here. When he gets here keep him here 'til I get back with the women."

"Goddam leg," Seth said. "I won't be much use."

"Keep that badge on Culpepper." Morgan took his own off. Seth frowned. "You want me to wear it into the Gorge?"

"No . . . but I'd like to think you'll hang on to it 'til this is over."

"I'm no lawman," Morgan said,. He tossed the tin star on the table.

"An' you got no ranch to defend," Seth added. "Without the badge, that makes you a hired gun. That's wrong no matter who hires you."

"You hired me. Same man. Same gun."

"It's different, Morgan, an' you know it."

"It's different to you, Seth. Not to me."

"You're a dyin' breed, Morgan . . . a damned poor shadow of your ol' daddy."

"Handy when the law needs me . . . a scourge on humanity when I refuse to wear a piece of tin." Morgan shook his head. "That don't make much sense to me."

"But you want me to keep the badge on Ephram Culpepper."

"Yeah . . . he's standing for you . . . I'm riding for Judge Barr."

"Bullshit! You're riding for Lee Morgan."

Morgan walked to the door and then turned back. "If that's true, Marshal, it wouldn't change just because I pinned on that tin star." He opened the door. "I'll be back . . . with the women."

Ephram Culpepper watched Morgan ride out. Then he walked back to the room where Seth was waiting. "Where's Morgan off to?"

"To bring back Strada's niece and the Barr girl." Ephram glanced at the table and saw the badge.

"Looks like you're short one deputy."

"You quittin' too?"

"I'll stand for you, Seth, 'til your leg ain't hurtin'."

"This'll likely as not be over with before that happens." Ephram grinned. "Well . . . preachin' and keepin' the peace seem to go together pretty good. Leastways . . . I'll give a try at it for a spell."

Morgan passed within five miles of Jude Bailey's place . . . and Tom Horn. Horn finally yielded to the Bailey's request that he stay the night and escort them back to Ketchum. It hadn't been his plan but with Blanchard's letter in his possession it might prove the wisest thing anyway.

Morgan was cold, tired and hungry but he pushed on until Pacer needed rest. He nosed out a line shack along the foothills of the Bitterroots and spent about three hours. It was almost dawn before he set out again. As he neared his destination, he began to hear gunfire. The source, which he found about fifteen minutes later, was another raid. This time on Jimmy Caleb's place. He saw the smoke and felt a new anger welling up inside but he knew there was nothing he could do. In fact, he rode even harder. It would be to his advantage to get to the Gorge when even more men were away.

It was near noon the following day when he finally

passed the outer perimeter and entered the rocky fortress. He was surprised to find Harvey Jessup still in camp and still in charge.

"We've been wondering about you," Jessup said. "Thought maybe I misjudged you."

"You didn't."

"You get Horn?"

"No . . . seems like that's not so important anymore." Jessup frowned. "Ran into Brock on the trail. He ordered me back here to pick up the women."

Jessup's face went a bit white. Morgan caught it in spite of the fact that Jessup did his best to cover it. "That right? You s'posed to meet 'im are you?" Morgan smelled a rat. He nodded. "Where?"

"Boise." It was a guess but it caught Jessup off guard.

"When, Morgan?"

"Soon as I can get there."

"An' he told you to bring both women?" Morgan thought it an odd question. On top of that, Jessup shifted his position a little.

"Yeah," Morgan replied, "why?" Jessup reached. He was fast. Lee Morgan was simply faster. The shot sounded like a cannon. Morgan knew that the results would be. He acted first. He threw open the shack's door and shouted for the men guarding the women. Both responded.

"What the hell happened?" one of them asked. He was looking past Morgan and into the shack.

"Jessup tried to kill me," Morgan replied. He holstered his gun. "I confronted him about the ambush he set up to get the Blanchard brothers."

The revelation got response. Obviously, both men knew about the men in Ketchum. It had been a long shot but Morgan reckoned that anyone put to guarding the hostages would have to be close to

Brock.

"You tellin' us the Blanchards got bushwhacked?"

"They did . . . and Jessup there," Morgan said, gesturing behind him with his thumb, "was responsible. Brock doesn't know who else Jessup might have on the inside. He sent me back for the women."

Morgan's statement brought much the same reaction as he'd gotten from Jessup. Something was not right. He'd have to gamble.

"The women?"

"The one that's left," Morgan said, easing his hand toward his hip. Each time he'd mentioned women, he'd gotten a strange response. He'd concluded, correctly, that one of the women was with Brock.

"He never said nothin' about it when he rode out."

"Why in hell should he?" Morgan snapped. "He didn't know it. He didn't know that son-of-a-bitch was gonna set up the Blanchards either. You want to argue with me . . . fine. You can explain it all to Brock yourself when he rides back in."

"No . . . I . . . I didn't mean that." The man looked in the shack again. "Jessup . . . Jeezus! I figured him all wrong."

"Money's a pretty good incentive," Morgan said, off-handedly. "Some o' these ranchers got plenty of it. Nothing would be better for them than to have a man on the inside."

"Yeah," the man said, pointing, "there was some of us figured it might be you."

"You were supposed to figure that," Morgan said, smiling. "The Big Boss wanted it that way."

"You work for . . ." Morgan held his breath. The man held his tongue. "Shit!" Morgan couldn't push it.

"Get the woman." The men nodded and disappeared around the corner. Several others had gathered nearby but now seemed to drift off, convinced of Morgan's validity. Fortunately, most of those with any reason to question him further were out of the compound. He wanted to be gone before they rode back in.

A minute later, the two guards showed up with Lileth Joy Johnson, Strada's niece. "Untie her," Morgan said. The man frowned. "You don't figure I can handle her?" The man cut the ropes. "Get a horse saddled and out front."

"I don't like your tone, Morgan. Who in hell made you the ramrod?"

Morgan shot a glance at Lil Johnson . . . a sort of silent apology. "Fuck you then," Morgan said. "I'll do it myself and take it up with Brock later."

"Yeah . . . yeah . . . we'll get the goddam horse." The door slammed.

"We're riding out," Morgan said, softly. "You'll be safe in a couple of hours. We're going to Ketchum. Just do as I tell you."

"They took Miss Barr. I heard some men talking. They said she was supposed to be taken to Boise."

"Shit," Morgan said, under his breath. Brock had something up his sleeve or the Mister Big in Boise did. "You got a heavy coat?" The girl shook her head. Morgan looked around and spotted Harv Jessup's sheepskin. He took it. "It'll be too big but you'll stay warm."

"I . . . I don't understand."

"Don't try right now. There'll be plenty of time on the trail. There's not a lot of that right now." The door opened. Morgan motioned to the girl and they walked past the two men without exchanging a word. Minutes later they were riding toward the trail that led out of Gunsmoke Gorge.

12

An icy blast of air poured down from Canada, across
the northern Montana glacier country and fanned
out east and west. The wind from the Bitterroots
carried it into Salmon Valley and it froze everything
in its path. Tom Horn had managed to keep just a
couple of hours head of it but the temperature
hovered near zero when he finally rode back into
Ketchum.

"You get Blanchard?" They were Seth Rawlings'
first words. Horn smiled. "I got 'im."

"Glad you're back."

"I was wonderin'."

"Morgan rode out . . . east. Thought you might
cross trails." Horn huddled near the pot belly and
rubbed his hands together, briskly. "We might
have, 'cept I was in a house. Rancher's place . . .
Jude Bailey."

"They hit Jude?"

"Nope . . . but Blanchard was readyin' himself
to." Horn fished out the letter he'd found and
handed it to Seth. By then, Ephram Culpepper was
stirring. "Bailey family rode in with me. We was
plannin' on waitin' another day but the weather
didn't look too fit."

Horn gestured toward the door. "Good thing we
moved out. Norther'll freeze ever' thin'." Horn

scratched his head. "Hope Morgan an' them women gits out of it."

"He will," Culpepper said, "if he gits out o' that hole in one piece." Culpepper extended his hand. "Glad to see you, Horn." They shook hands and Culpepper set about to make some coffee.

Seth Rawlings read the letter . . . first to himself and then out loud.

"You make anythin' of it, Marshal?" Tom Horn asked.

"Some. Some's easy. The R B here . . . that's the Rocky Barr ranch."

"Yeah, I figured that part. What I couldn't figure was what he meant when he said . . . what is it . . ."

"*We have it*, is what he wrote," Seth looked up. "That don't figure. Judge Barr has been the toughest holdout in the valley."

"Unless he's buckled up since Morgan took his daughter in."

"Don't hardly seem possible," Marshal Rawlings replied. "Morgan told me that fella Brock was s'posed to be gone fer a week. Now by my reckonin' . . . that'd be a trip to Boise. Figured he'd likely find out what he's supposed to do an' then contact Judge Barr."

"Yeah," Horn agreed, "but Blanchard had this letter more'n two weeks ago . . . a'fore Morgan ever took Barr's daughter in." Seth looked down and scanned the letter again. "Well, this here F Q is easy enough," he looked up at Tom, "that'd be the Four Queens . . . Belle Moran's place."

"An' the feller what wrote it . . . that there T Y?"

"No ideas," Seth said. "Not even a good guess." Ephram Culpepper poured three cups of coffee, moved a chair up near the stove and sat down. "Looks like one of us got some ridin' to do, Horn . . .

to Boise.''

"Morgan said to sit tight 'til he come in with the women.'' Ephram grinned. "You takin' orders from Lee Morgan now, Seth?''

"No goddam it,'' Seth replied, irritably, "but maybe he'll know somethin' else from one o' the women . . . or from somebody up in the Gorge.''

"That's if'n he gets back at all,'' Ephram said.

"He'll make it.'' Ephram looked up at Tom Horn. He smiled.

"I didn't mean if'n somebody took 'im out, Horn. I meant he might have to git out o' this weather.''

"That he will,'' Seth agreed. "Especially with two gals fer saddle companions.''

The door opened and all three men came up with weapons. The door closed, the man stomped his feet, pulled the neck scarf down and removed his hat. They were looking at Judge Isaac Barr.

Lil Johnson was shivering almost uncontrollably. She was curled into a ball, back against the outside wall of the dilapidated line shack. Lee Morgan struggled to clear the drifted snow from in front of the door.

"Can w . . . w . . . we build a fire?'' she asked.

"If there's wood,'' Morgan said. He stopped digging and looked up at her. "I've got some coffee too.'' She smiled, weakly and nodded. The wind, sharp as a straight edge, was out of the northeast. Morgan tethered the animals on the southwest side of the shack. He wasn't certain of their exact location but he was guessing the shack was on Josh Killerman's Rocking K spread.

Morgan finally forced the door and the couple got inside. The furnishings were sparse. A tick mattress, without a bed frame, a small table with one broken chair and a #7 cook stove. Several 2 x 4 and 2 x 12 boards made up some cupboard space. It was empty, save for a coal oil lamp about a third full. Morgan pointed and smiled. "Light and firewood," he said.

Twenty minutes later, the shack, in spite of its flimsy construction, was warm and cozy. Lil set about to make coffee and warm two tins of beans. Morgan ventured into the cold again in search of more wood. They ate in silence with Morgan finally breaking it as he rolled a smoke.

"You hear anything else when Brock took Miss Barr away?" Lil shook her head. She sat, legs pulled beneath her, near the stove. Both hands were wrapped around the tin cup and she blew, gently, at the steaming contents. "You still cold?"

"Inside," she said, "with fear."

"You're safe now. We both are."

"We're out of that camp . . . yes . . . but *safe?* I wish I'd never come to this god-forsaken land." Morgan frowned. "Oh . . . I'm no pioneer woman . . . I haven't the stomach or the backbone for it. My parents are dead and gone. They . . . they burned to death. My mother was Ben Strada's sister. The only family on either side still alive. I was not yet of age so . . ."

"So here you are." She nodded. Morgan winced. How could he tell her that she no longer had an uncle either. "I hate to bring it up, but we'll have to ride out before daylight. I don't want to run the risk of being spotted."

"I understand. I just want to get home . . . that's all." They finished their coffee and Morgan put the last big log in the stove.

"That'll burn down in a couple of hours. There isn't anymore. I'll bust up the table and chair in the morning. We'll at least get warm and have some coffee before we ride out. You take the mattress and both coats. I've got my bedroll.''

Morgan's whole body ached. He hadn't realized how dog tired he really was and how much he ached in every bone and joint. He stirred only when he felt the press of weight atop him. Cold air rushed into the gap in the bedroll and he blinked awake.

"I'm freezing," Lil Johnson said. She had opened the gap and was slipping between the top cover and Morgan's body. She was naked! He heard the crackling of a fire and glanced at the stove. She had started another fire with the chair. Half her lithe, young body was visible in the dancing light from the flames.

"You sure you want it this way?" She answered with a kiss . . . a heavy, passionate kiss. Her tongue darted into Morgan's mouth. He was surprised at her expertise.

Her breasts were small but firm and the nipples, hardened in the cold of the shack, seemed nearly as big as the breasts themselves. She scooted down and brushed them along Morgan's lips. He moaned softly.

Lil slipped still farther into the bedroll and began undoing Morgan's belt. By the time she had stripped him, he had responded to her efforts and his own desires. His mind was filled with contradictions but Lil Johnson's mouth around his blood gorged shaft quickly dulled his thinking processes.

"Love me," she whispered, "love me and I'll do anything you ask." Morgan thought it almost humorous. It was Lileth who was doing the love-making . . . and in ways which Morgan would probably not have had the courage to ask . . . at least the first time around.

Her hands caressed his body, exploring, stroking, pausing at the most sensitive junctures. He found her breasts and stroked and pulled at them. Lil's hips were soon gyrating atop his groin . . . and she rubbed along his shaft . . . back and forth. He could feel the moisture of her arousal.

She was on her knees, her head was thrown back and her eyes closed in a delirium of ecstacy. Suddenly, she stopped. Her breathing was heavy, almost labored. She leaned foward. "I . . . I've *never* . . . not completely . . . not with . . . with a man . . . just . . . just a boy I knew. We just . . . touched."

"Jeezus," Lee whispered. He doubted that Lil even heard him. He nodded. He moved her from atop him, layed her down and began kissing her. He let his hands wander over her body while his tongue and lips worked along her neck, breasts, stomach and finally to the very center of her emerging womanhood.

"There'll be a little pain . . . a kind of sharp, burning pain . . . just for a second," he said. Their eyes met. She smiled and nodded. Morgan entered her with all the care and finesse he'd acquired. Even he was surprised at the minimal resistance her hymen offered. Lil's only reaction was a slight stiffening, a frown on her face and the gentle biting of her lower lip. A moment later . . . her face seemed radiant with a pleasure she had never known.

Morgan pumped with a measured rhythm . . . continuing his gentle caresses and kissing. He was about to burst and had to struggle againt the temptation of pleasing only himself. Slowly she began to respond. Her body joined his own in the age old, pleasure filled motion of male and female . . . once again a single entity of creation.

"Oh it's good . . . oh God . . . it's so good . . . oh

Morgan . . . God . . . oooh God . . . oh GOD!'' Lil's climactic reaction came upon her so suddenly even she wasn't ready. Morgan, caught unaware, quickly recovered. They reached the peak of ecstacy together, hovering for a moment and then collapsing into each other's arms and the void which follows the summit of human contact.

Morgan added a few final pieces of wood to the dying fire and then rolled a smoke. He slipped into the bedroll next to Lil. He thought she was asleep. She turned on her side and kissed his cheek.

"Thank you," she said. "You were very gentle . . . I . . . I somehow knew you would be."

"No regrets?"

"No regrets. I was a girl . . . now I'm a woman. Only a man can make that possible . . . not a boy."

Judge Barr's sudden appearance in Ketchum proved even more a surprise to Seth Rawlings than he had, at first, imagined. Seth assumed that Barr was looking for him and by sheer luck had found him. Neither was the case. Rawlings quickly brought Judge Barr up to date on events.

"I'm glad you're here, Horn," Barr said. "I've brought money and tomorrow I'll pay you off."

"Haven't really don't the job yet," Horn said.

"You've done all there is to do . . . it's over. I'm here because of this." Judge Barr produced a letter. Seth Rawlings read it . . . aloud.

> Judge,
> Your daughter and Ben Strada's niece will both be returned to you . . . unharmed, when you comply with the instructions set down herein. Contact all the ranch owners. Gather them . . . with

yourself, in Ketchum. Be there no later
than Thursday night. My people will
meet with you Friday. If all goes well . . .
you will see the women safely returned.

                                    Brock

The old marshal studied the page and then handed
it to Tom Horn. "That look familiar?" Horn glanced
at it and nodded. Judge Barr frowned.

"You mean you got a similar letter? That's why
you're all here?"

"A similar letter," Horn said, "same hand writin'
. . . not to us but to Jess Blanchard. Come out o'
Boise . . . an' come out at a time when this here fella
Brock couldn't o' wrote it." Horn handed Judge
Barr both his letter and the letter Horn had taken
from Jess Blanchard's body.

"I . . . I don't understand."

Ephram Culpepper now looked at both letters.
"Looks to me like you been dealt a crooked hand,
Judge." He glanced at Marshal Rawlings. Seth
nodded his agreement.

"They pull every ranch owner left all into one nice
little bunch."

"Move in from both directions," Tom said. "That
outfit out o' Picabo an' the main bunch from the
Gorge. Sounds like they figger to do in Ketchum the
same as ol' Quantrill did down Kansas way back in
sixty-four."

"An ambush?" Judge Barr looked down. He
paced, rubbed his forehead and then studied the
letters again. "You're saying that this man Brock
didn't write these?"

"Couldn't have . . . leastways not accordin' to Lee
Morgan. Brock was nowhere near Boise an' we've

got that kid locked up across the street. He confirms that there's somebody bigger'n Brock involved.''

"Then I've asked all these men to ride in here to their deaths . . . just to save my daughter and Ben Strada's niece. Now . . . God . . . even Ben is . . .''

"What did you tell them?'' Seth asked. The judge looked up, quizzically. "The other owners? What did you tell them?''

"I . . . oh God . . . I *lied.* I didn't want to risk being turned down. I told them we had a plan . . . a good plan and . . . and *help* on the way.''

"Too late to do much about that,'' Ephram said. "Hell . . . they'll be here tomorrow. I figger them maraudin' bastards will hit Friday.'' He looked at Tom Horn. "How many you guess Tom?''

"Seventy . . . eighty mebbe . . . in both batches.''

Judge Barr leaped to his feet. "I've got to ride out . . . warn the others.'' He reached for his coat. Tom Horn caught his arm.

"Judge . . . hold on. Where you plannin' on startin'? East? West mebbe . . . or should you ride north first?'' The judge quickly recognized the futility of his thought. He slumped into a chair.

"I'll have to order a complete evacuation of the town,'' Seth said, "at first light. I hope you two will help. Organize the town's folk an' git 'em out o' here. I'll stay behind and try to talk sense to the ranch owners as they ride in.''

"I'll stick, Marshal,'' Horn said. They both looked at Ephram. He nodded. "If'n I figger 'im right. . . Lee Morgan oughta be ridin' in sometime tomorrow . . . hopefully with them gals . . . your daughter should be safe, Judge.''

Judge Isaac Barr looked up. There were tears in his eyes and an expression on his face which took all three men by surprise. He got to his feet, walked to the table and picked up the two letters. He read them both, held them up and studied each with care. His face paled.

"My God!" He put the letters down. His hand was trembling. "I . . . I think I know who wrote these," he said. His voice was soft now . . . he pushed to get more volume. He was choked up. "The initial . . . the T and the Y . . . they . . . they were short for a ranch name a few years back. The Yellow. It was called the Yellow. The whole name was the Yellow Pine ranch." Marshal Seth Rawlings' jaw dropped.

"Tom Yeager's place?" Seth nodded in confirmation of his own question and its answer. "Jeezus . . . it makes sense." He looked at Ephram and Tom. "Thomas Seaton Yeager . . . United States Senator. He's been fightin' for mineral rights in Idaho for years. Struck some gold up on his place . . . got hisself in some trouble last election time. Accused o' sneakin' around other folk's property . . . checkin' fer gold . . . silver . . . copper. He got out of it . . . got re-elected but they was plenty o' noise about it."

"Jehosophat! A Yewnited States Senator? You sure about this, Judge?" Judge Barr looked up, slowly. Tears filled his eyes. He nodded.

Seth Rawlings worked his way over and sat down next to Judge Isaac Barr. "Isaac . . . are you sure?"

"I should have recognized the hand sooner . . . I've seen it enough times." He looked into Seth's eyes. "He wanted me to recognize it . . . didn't he?"

"Prob'ly," Seth replied, weakly. He shook his head and then looked up at the others.

"Tom Yeager has been comin' out to the Rocky Barr fer a good long time now. Courtin' Morgana. They planned on gettin' hitched up next spring."

"The girl . . . does she . . ."

"Know?" Tom nodded. "Can't be sure . . . but it'd

seem likely."

"If that's the case," Ephram said, "then Lee Morgan's a dead man."

Morgan was cold enough to be dead but there, the similiarity ended. He and Lil rode out of the line shack well before dawn. Their horses struggled with the off trail snow. Morgan couldn't risk running into the returning marauders. Brock or most anyone else. He ordered that they ride an hour . . . then walk a half hour to give the mounts a rest. They were not making the time he'd hoped for however and, after their latest stop, he decided to risk a return to the main trail.

Some six hours after they'd ridden from the line shack, Morgan and Lileth Johnson rounded a curve in the road and spotted a buggy. Morgan, throwing caution to the wind, fired a shot in the air. Moments later, they came face to face with Josh Killerman.

They exchanged information and Morgan was clearly concerned about the turn of events. Nonetheless, he felt the only option open to them was to reach Ketchum. He freed himself of the slow pace of his trip by leaving Lil with Killerman. Then, he gave Pacer his head.

Seth Rawlings had come to the conclusion that there was no end to the surprises he'd been getting. At just after four o'clock the door opened and Lee Morgan walked through it.

"I'll be damned," Seth said. "I figgered you was dead . . . sure."

"Not yet," Morgan said. He moved to the stove and poured himself some coffee. "Ran into Josh Killerman coming in. Strada's niece is with him now. They'll be here tonight. Killerman told me . . ."

"I know what he told you . . . an' why." Seth told

Morgan what had happened. Horn, Culpepper and
Isaac Barr were even then rounding up Ketchum's
populace and readying them to move out. They were
getting plenty of resistance. Morgan had about
decided to join them in the effort when Addie
Terhune walked in. She looked straight at Morgan.

"I didn't know you were back but it's a good
thing." She stepped aside and in walked Belle
Moran from Boise. She looked stern.

"What the hell are you doing here?"

"Where's Judge Barr," she asked.

"Trying to round up some citizens, why?"

"You'd best get him," Belle said, "and anybody
else that owns anything hereabouts. I rode in to
warn you." Morgan nodded and left the office.

The decision was made to bring together the
area's ranch owners and the citizens of Ketchem
that night at Addie's place. Both Seth Rawling and
Judge Barr protested the idea at the outset. They
felt strongly that the families should clear out but
Tom Horn found a solution to the disagreement. He
suggested that the decision be left to those affected.
The vote was to meet that night.

Belle found Lee Morgan at a corner table. He had
a bottle and a glass and he had just rolled a smoke.

"You want company?"

"Why not?"

"Does the judge know *everything?*"

"All he needs to know, I'd guess. Is Morgana solid
with Yeager?" Belle nodded. "Has been all along.
That's why she agreed to come with you so easy."

"How come she didn't turn me in to Brock?"

"From what I could find out, Brock didn't know
about her. Nobody did 'cept her an' the good
senator. She finally told him but . . . well, by then
you'd already got in an' out again with Strada's

niece."

"You got any kind of a head count on their men?"

"More'n hundred," Belle said. "They'll burn this place to the ground an' kill anybody they find. Don't recall ever seein' a man with the gold fever as bad as Yeager's got it. He's crazy."

"I thought he was in pretty good shape."

"Ever'body did. That's 'cause he was . . . once. He stuck ever'thing into a railroad venture. He got conned. He used his office to get a lot of big cattle-men involved but he had to promise rail transport out of Idaho . . . same as it is down in Wyoming an' Kansas an' Nebraska. Hell . . . even Montana is in better shape. When that fell through . . . he was in big trouble."

"An' those cattlemen *still* don't know?"

Belle shook her head. "With his power, Yeager's been able to stall 'em but he needs cash. A lot of cash an' in a big hurry. A lot of mining rights are government owned. He can't do much with those but if he's got access to the land around them, he can come out of it."

"You mean sell the access rights to the big mineral outfits?"

"As best I can get the story . . . yeah." She smiled. "The son-of-a-bitch even had me boxed up and wrapped. I believed what he said."

"Which was?"

"Talk a woman likes to hear . . . particularly one like me. I fell for it like some little virgin farm girl."

"You didn't know about Morgana Barr?"

"Not then." Belle downed a drink. She winced and shivered. "How do you stop somethin' as big as Yeager?"

"I don't know for sure," Morgan said. He leaned forward. "Hell, maybe you *don't*."

"Somebody's gotta *try*."

"Cemeteries are full o' folks that *tried*."

"You quittin'?"

"It's not up to me." Morgan gestured around the room. "It's up to the people that fill this place tonight. Idaho is theirs."

"An' what do you get out o' helpin' 'em, Morgan?"

"I'm here. The Spade Bit is gone. I guess I owe some'thin' to somebody for that."

"And then what?"

Morgan smiled. "Good question, Belle. According to Seth Rawlings, I'm an antique. A poor imitation of my daddy . . . lived past my time."

"Hell . . . you're not that old."

"No . . . but Seth is right. For *who* I am . . . *where* I come from and *what* I am . . . well, I guess I should be in some eastern museum or maybe old Bill Cody's *Wild West Show*."

"Bull! If the men comin' west now are all like Tom Yeager . . . this country needs you bad . . . you an' Tom Horn an' a thousand more like you."

"Maybe . . . but it won't happen. No, I'll end up hanging from a tree, or get shot on some dusty street, or bushwhacked on some back trail. Horn too."

"That's a poor way to go out."

Morgan looked up and smiled. "Not so bad maybe. Beats hell out of Cody's Wild West Show. Or Barnum's Dime Museum. I don't want to end up throwin' in my hand in some damned fancy, eastern boarding house."

"Why don't you come to work for me?"

"Pimpin' or shootin' people?"

"Goddam, Morgan, you're an ungrateful bastard."

"I don't mean anything by it, Belle. I appreciate it. Your heart's in the right place. It's just that what you're offerin' is no different really than back east."

"Well . . . mebbe we're both just spittin' into the wind. Might end right here . . . right in Ketchum, Idaho. Gunsmoke an' blood soaked snow. Make great writin' for Ned Buntline or somebody like 'im."

"Gun fighter and the whore," Morgan said, grinning, "that it, Belle?"

"I had something a little more refined in mind. The lady and the shootist maybe." Morgan laughed. Belle Moran poured them both a drink and they proposed a silent toast.

13

Dawn came to Ketchum like a fragile piece of crystal. Ice clung to the trees, telegraph wires, windows and anything made of metal which was exposed. The air was as still and cold as death itself. The only sign of life was a single curl of blue-black smoke belching from the chimney at Addie Terhune's palace of pleasure.

Brock stood in his stirrups and surveyed the scene below. Behind him, fifty-five men sat their mounts, cold, irritable and more than ready to raze the quiet, mountain town.

"I don't give a goddamn about anybody down there," he said, "except Lee Morgan. If he's there I want the son-of-a-bitch alive. I don't care that he's shot up first but I want the pleasure of finishing the job." He looked at the man next to him. "You got that?" The man nodded.

Opposite Brock's position, a little to the south and east of Ketchum, a gunman and bounty hunter named Jace Kileen headed up a band of forty men. Of the force at Tom Yeager's disposal, these two groups represented all but twenty-two men. A dozen of those had simply ridden out . . . either too good to participate in such a slaughter . . . or simply too yellow. The remaining ten stayed with Senator Thomas Yeager in Boise.

At Brock's signal—a single rifle shot—both hands would converge on Ketchum. Anything or anyone in their respective paths was subject to destruction. Their target was Addie's place and the people they believed were in it. All of the ranch owners from a hundred to a hundred fifty miles around.

Down along the main street, hidden from view inside second floor rooms or up on roof tops, were thirty-five ranch owners. Among them, acting as their leaders, was Judge Isaac Barr and Josh Killerman. These men, mostly pioneer stock who had fought Indians and outlaws most of their time in Idaho, were the cream of the crop available. Most were good rifle shots and none of them were strangers to fear.

Ketchum's main street ran north and south. At the south end, huddled in the blacksmith's shop, was Lee Morgan and a half a dozen of the town's men. They too were men who could use weapons . . . at least with some skill. On the opposite end of the street, Marshal Seth Rawling waited with five more such men. Lined up in front of Seth and his men were half a dozen plungers all wired to dynamite. There were four rows of it, about ten feet apart, stretching along the street from one side to the other. At the far end of the main street, Morgan had a similar set-up.

In between them, with the heaviest concentration of explosives placed right in the street's center, was Ephram Culpepper. He was heavily armed . . . alone save for his woman who would load for him. He had a single plunger in front of him. Between them, the set-up had taken to within an hour of dawn. Several things they wanted to do had to be abandoned. The lookouts returned with word that the marauders were riding in.

West of Ketchum, ready to move out—and with luck—catch the stragglers, were the bulk of Ketchum's citizenry. About sixty merchants, barbers, drovers and a few miners. Leading them was Tom Horn.

Everyone had gathered the night before at Addie Terhune's place. They drank and listened. They listened to Judge Isaac Barr and to Seth Rawlings. They listened even to Belle Moran and Tom Horn. Finally, Lee Morgan spoke to them. If they let others destroy Ketchum and drive them out, they were finished, he told them. If it must be destroyed . . . let them do it . . . destroy the plague which threatened it along with the town and then rebuild bigger, better and stronger.

By two o'clock—working in shifts and with the women keeping hot coffee and food ready—the men had rounded up dynamite, weapons and ammunition. They acted according to plans formulated by Rawlings, Horn and Morgan. The women and children were housed in Culpepper's church—the only building with a basement. Now . . . they were ready.

Brock slipped his rifle from the scabbard, raised it above his head, reached up and levered a shell into the chamber and pulled the trigger. The men moved out. Slowly at first . . . then their mounts broke into a trot, a gallop and finally . . . full-fledged run. Their timing was nearly perfect, both groups reaching their respective ends of town almost simultaneously. By now, the lead men had begun to shout and they were shooting into every building.

The din was deafening. Shots, the shattering glass, the old rebel yells, Indian war-whoops and plain old, cowpoke yah-hooing. Morgan and

Rawlings waited . . . waited . . . waited. The lead men
were nearing the center of the town. Others were
strung out behind them, all the way to the street's
end.

"Now," Morgan said. The men behind him pushed
down.

"Now," Seth Rawlings said. The men behind him
pushed down. There had been no time to bury the
explosives. Indeed, even had there been the time,
the ground was steel hard. Some of the dynamite
was pulled from its wiring by the horse's hooves. It
would not detonate for all of it was simply buried
beneath the snow. That aside, much of it did go up.

Horses and men alike were ripped to shreds.
Limbs were torn from bodies and men flew through
the air like so many rag dolls. There were screams as
huge holes were torn in the street and the snow
turned from a pure white to a pale pink and then to a
scarlet.

Fifteen to twenty riders reached the center of
town . . . escaping the explosives behind them. Three
or four—the most astute among them—dismounted
and rushed for the safety of nearby buildings. The
others milled about atop the last of the charges.
Ephram Culpepper shoved down the handle of his
plunger. Eight men died instantly.

The roar of the dynamite faded. Now, from either
side of the street, a fusillade of rifle fire poured down
upon the still breathing but hapless victims. Inside
Addie Terhune's saloon, a woman screamed. She
was Ephram Culpepper's woman. She died
screaming.

Ephram whirled and saw two men . . . one of whom
had just killed the woman. He fired two shots from
his Winchester. Both men died. Ephram got to his
feet, walked back and knelt beside his woman. He

had tears in his eyes. He heard a noise. He looked up. There stood Brock.

Brock was as fast a man as Ephram had ever faced. Both had been momentarily distracted by a noise above them. They glanced up at the same time. Addie Terhune was there! She wasn't supposed to be. She was holding a shotgun. Brock drew. Ephram's arm was still sore . . . stiff . . . slow to react. Brock's shot passed through the fleshy part of Ephram's left shoulder just below the armpit. Ephram winced but even wounded, his draw was fast and accurate. Brock took a shot between the eyes.

"Ephram . . . my God . . . look out!" Ephram whirled. A shot rang out. . . loud even amidst the outside rifle fire. Ephram saw the man. Big . . . sinister looking. He was holding a smoking .44. Ephram heard the crack of wood behind him. He turned in time to see Addie Terhune's body smash into the top of the bar. It cracked and then slipped from sight. Ephram wheeled. The sinister man had holstered the gun. He was grinning.

"Hello, Preacher Man."

"Jace Kileen . . you rotten son-of-a-bitch."

"I'll cross draw you, Preacher Man . . . since you're hit an' all." Ephram holstered his gun. He realized his throat was dry. *Jeezus*, he thought, *I'm scared.* He'd seen Jace Kileen. He'd never seen a man faster. Ephram's right hand tightened into a fist, relaxed and tightened again. He swallowed, wet his lips, relaxed his hand and drew.

The barrel of his gun was clear of the holster. The shot travelled at an angle and the shell buried itself in a table leg. Ephram's mouth rippled with a grin. It opened but there was no sound. Jace Kileen put a bullet between Ephram Culpepper's eyes.

Perhaps a dozen of the marauders tried to make it back the way they had come . . . from the south. Morgan was there . . . he and the men with him cut them down. Twenty—perhaps even thirty—some wounded, managed to gather, find mounts and ride north. Seth Rawlings let them pass. He'd seen Tom Horn and Ketchum's citizens coming up from the west. The marauders rode straight into half of them. The others, with Horn leading, flanked them about a minute later. Most fell to the ground, hands up, quitting at last.

There were stragglers . . . eight all told. One of them was Jace Kileen. The others scattered. Jace rode hard and fast straight toward Boise. The fight was over. Twenty minutes . . . perhaps a half an hour. No one, not even the participants, could be certain . . . but it *was* over.

Seth, Tom Horn and Lee Morgan met in Addie's place. The evidence told the story . . . or most of it. What remained they learned from Addie's one-armed barkeep, Louie Mathers.

"The preacher . . . he . . . he shot that fella," Louis said, pointing to Brock, "but . . . I never seen a man so fast as the other one. Preacher Man called him . . . uh, Jace . . . Jace Kileen."

Morgan reloaded, picked up the Winchester he'd loaned to Culpepper and headed for the door.

"Where the hell you bound for?" Seth yelled.

"Boise."

"Morgan!" Lee stopped and turned around. Seth Rawlings handed Tom Horn a badge. "You took it off this mornin'. I'm askin' you to put it on, Horn, and ride to Boise with me—as *law*." Morgan frowned and then scowled at Tom Horn.

Tom smiled . . . that old, soft, friendly smile of his.

He shrugged. "May as well do it right," he said, taking the badge. Now, both men looked at Morgan. Seth reached in his pocket and withdrew another badge. He held it out. Again, Morgan's eyes met those of the old manhunter . . . Tom Horn.

"Shit," Morgan said. He walked over, took the badge and jammed it into his pocket. Just then, Josh Killerman walked through the door.

"Can't find Judge Barr nowhere."

"You got a head count on our side yet?"

"Five men so far." Killerman saw Ephram. He shook his head. "Six."

"The judge is prob'ly at the church." Killerman shook his head.

"Checked there first . . . I . . . I think he rode out for Boise."

"Jeezus," Morgan said. He pushed by Killerman and raced out.

"Somebody needs to stay here an' take charge," Tom said.

"Yeah," Seth agreed. He pulled another badge out and handed it to Josh Killerman. "You're deputized. Take over here." Tom smiled and the two hurried out.

The trio stopped at the Rocky Barr ranch. They were all certain Judge Barr would have made the same stop. They were wrong. Nonetheless, they took the time to stock up for the trip, tell the judge's foreman and his men what had happened and to rest up. Somewhere, the old judge would have to stop as well. Boise was too long a ride without rest.

Senator Tom Yeager had made quite a show for the voters in Boise. He promised them an end to the land troubles in Idaho and to the killer marauders who'd been plaguing them for months. He also made it appear he'd quit Boise to return to Washington. In fact, he was holed up in Belle Moran's private quarters in the Four Queens.

"Senator, I don't think you can expect anything this soon from Ketchum. It's a long ride in the best of weather." Yeager looked up at the well dressed man who had been serving him as a personal aide for some eight years. A former Pinkerton agent, his name was Ted Peabody.

"You still don't grasp what's happened do you, Ted? That bitch! That whore Belle. She left word at Tate Bosley's office and now I found out she rode off to Ketchum to warn them."

"Sheriff Bosley will pose no problem. I've handled that, I told you about it. He was out of town and the minute he rides in . . . uh . . . the situation will be settled. As to the woman warning someone in Ketchum . . ." the man smiled, "*who?* And what good would it do. We've nearly a hundred men to handle that."

"You can reassure me all you want to Ted . . . but until I see that whore's body . . . hers . . . and Bosley's . . . and the others . . . I won't . . . I *can't* rest easy. You seem to forget what's at stake here."

"Not at all, Senator, but perhaps you're underestimating the men I've assigned to do this job."

"Ted . . . . Goddam you . . . don't try to soft soap me anymore. I turned this whole thing to you a year and a half ago. Now, by God, I'm here in person . . ."

"They proved to be tougher than I thought. I'll admit that but it's under control now . . . settled."

"Too many people know . . . two many are involved. Tom Horn! Good God . . . ten years ago, he was a national hero. Seth Rawlings! One of the finest and oldest lawmen west of the Mississippi. And this . . ."

"Morgan?"

"Yes . . . yes . . . Lee Morgan. I've heard plenty about *him*."

"The son of some old time gunman or other. No real threat."

"You'd better be right Ted—about *everything*." The door opened and one of Ted's men came in. He looked stern. Yeager looked from one to the other.

"*Well?*"

The man closed the door. "Sheriff Bosley . . . he . . . he's back. He arrested six of our men. He's got a half a dozen deputies and he's comin' *here*." Yeager's face paled. Even Ted Peabody reeled under the shock of the news.

"Another one you underestimated. Is that it, *Ted?*"

The other men? Where are they?"

"Gone . . . 'cept fer that gunny they call Cody."

"*Gone?* Where in hell did they *go?*"

"Rode out. I'm doin' the same." Ted Peabody reached into his coat, withdrew a Colt's model Deringer and put a single bullet into the man's head.

"Ted . . . for God's sake . . . we can't kill them all." Ted Peabody dragged the man's body to a closet, shoved it inside and closed the door. He straightened.

"Tom," he said, his voice low but firm . . . almost steely . . . "don't whine. I can't stand your whining. I've come a long way with you . . . I've got more at stake than you have. You're *somebody* . . . I'm just hired help. Now shut up, Senator . . . and I'll get us both out of this."

Both men heard the door and turned toward it. It opened and Jace Kileen walked in. He quickly explained what had happened in Ketchum.

"Those that know about you," Kileen said, "will

be here. Most still don't. You want to keep it that
way?"

"Of course he does," Ted Peabody said. Kileen
ignored Peabody. Tom Yeager finally nodded.
"Kileen . . . I need you here to do a job." Again, the
gunman ignored Peabody and spoke directly to
Yeager.

"Cody told me, downstairs, that the law is onto
you. They'll be here in a few minutes. Now me an'
Cody will stand with you . . . for a price."

"Name it."

"To start," Kileen said, smiling and pointing at
Ted. "I want his job." Ted Peabody was incredu-
lous. He jerked his head and looked at Senator
Yeager.

Yeager's eyes never left Kileen's. "Take it," he
said, coldly. Ted Peabody reached. His hand never
got near his coat. Kileen shot him in the forehead.

"What else?" Yeager asked, his voice shaky.

"We'll settle that later. Just make certain you're
here." Kileen walked out, walked down the stairs
and had just reached the main floor when Tate
Bosley and his men walked in. Two of them stopped
dead in their tracks.

"Tate . . . that's . . . that's Jace Kileen."

"You're under arrest," Tate said. He was carrying
a shotgun and he raised the barrel until it was
leveled at Kileen. The man to Tate's right glanced
around the room. Everyone had moved back save a
young man at the bar. He downed a shot of whiskey,
set the glass on the bar and both arms moved like
whips. Jace Kileen dropped to one knee, drawing
with a speed which defied description. Tate Bosley,
Sheriff of Boise for more than eight years, died
instantly. So did his two chief deputies. Outside,
two more fled. Neither got out of sight.

"Do we bust them others out o' jail," Cody asked

Kileen.

"No need. There'll be three men riding into Boise." Kileen smiled. "Seth Rawlings is one of 'em, an' I've got an old account to settle with him." He looked at the kid named Cody. "You can have yourself a whole new reputation with the second one —old Tom Horn."

"Shit!" Cody grinned and gripped the butts of his twin Colt's.

"Who's the other one?"

"Heard his name kicked around," Kileen said, "but I don't know anything about him. Name's Morgan . . . Lee Morgan."

"I'll be waitin' right here," Cody said. Kileen nodded and went back upstairs.

"The sheriff is dead. No one else will bother you. The ones riding in from Ketchum Cody and I will handle. After that . . . I'll tell you what else I want."

"Get the job done, Kileen . . . that's all. Just get it done. I'll see to it you're well payed."

The Rocky Barr ranch was the end of the line for Seth Rawlings. Back in Ketchum, his leg had not been too important. He really didn't have to use it that much. The ride proved more than it could take. It ripped open and bled badly. Seth elicited a promise that both Tom Horn and Lee Morgan would honor their commitments and act for the law. They both agreed.

They arrived in Boise in the early hours of the morning. They rode to the sheriff's office and found it abandoned and the cells empty. Petie Wheeler limped up just as they were leaving. He motioned for them to follow him inside.

"You gents ride in from Ketchum?" They were surprised. "Plenty o' talk circulatin' about it. Most excitement in Boise in twenty year or more." Petie had been the general clean-up man and cook at the jail. He'd worked the entire time for Tate Bosley. He told Tom and Lee what had happened.

"Them other two deputies . . . hell fire . . . they rode out o' here like somebody put horse linament on their peters. Little later . . . this here kid . . . totes two Colt's . . . he come by an' turned ever'body loose. They was six. Four o' them high-tailed it too."

"What about the others?"

"Went back over to the Queens. They got it all to themselves."

"You know who all is in there?"

"Best I can figger . . . this kid . . . two o' them what he let out an' Jace Kileen." Tom Horn let out a long, low whistle. Morgan eyed him.

"He the old bounty hunter?" Morgan asked.

"No older'n me," Tom said.

"I thought he was dead. I figured that old barkeep back in Ketchum was wrong."

"Yeah . . . I kinda thought mebbe he was too, but he wasn't."

"This Kileen . . . he was good."

"The best," Tom said.

"Better than my dad?"

"I don't know if there was *any* man *better* than Buckskin Frank Leslie. But there were a few around just as good. One of 'em killed him."

"Yeah . . . Harv Logan."

"Well . . . Jace Kileen was right up there with all of 'em."

"You scared of him, Tom?"

"You damned right I am. I get a chance I'll take him out with the Creedmoor."

"It's not that kind of a fight Tom," Morgan said. "You take your shotgun and you take out those others . . . two of 'em anyway. I can't say what this kid Cody will be like."

"Uh huh . . . an' you'll take Kileen?"

"I want Yeager and I don't want Judge Barr gettin' killed." Morgan turned to Petie Wheeler. "You know who Judge Isaac Barr is . . . by sight I mean?"

"Yep."

"You seen him?"

"Nope."

"Morgan . . . I've come to like you, boy . . . seen you work too. You're good . . ."

"But not good enough to take Jace Kileen . . . is that what you're leading up to?"

"That's about it."

"You got a better way? They won't come out and trail us and I don't know anybody else close by that'll go in after 'em. If we don't, Yeager gets away clean—with everything. Folks in Ketchum don't win."

"You're tellin' me ever'thing I don't want to hear, son. It's all right o' course, but I still don't want to hear it." Tom Horn walked out. Morgan frowned. Surely the old man hunter hadn't quit him. In a moment, Tom returned. He was toting his Parker shotgun.

"When?" he asked.

"In the morning," Morgan answered. "I'd like to find Judge Barr." Morgan looked around the office. "We can stay right here."

Morgan looked down at old Petie Wheeler. The old man was frowning. He wasn't certain of this young, dark eyed gunman. Morgan reached into his coat pocket, felt around and withdrew a tin star. He held it up, shook his head and then pinned it on his coat lapel. Tom Horn grinned. Petie Wheeler grinned. He shook his head.

"I'll be back in an hour," Morgan said.

14

Lee Morgan woke with a start. He wasn't exactly certain why. The only noise was the occasional snoring spells of Tom Horn. Morgan got up, turned up the lamp and rolled himself a smoke. It was nearly three o'clock in the morning. He sat down and looked over at Tom Horn. He couldn't help but wonder if he'd live that long.

His mind wandered back over the years—the years and the few miles from Boise to the old Spade Bit ranch. The day he'd come back. Scared. Knowing he'd failed. Trying to ride with the likes of Butch and Sundance and Harvey Logan. Logan! God. He was fast. Morgan's face wrinkled up as he remembered the day in the cook shack at the Spade Bit.

Lee walked in . . . bound on turning and trying Harvey Logan. Old McCorkle the cook was busy at his stove. Wait! It wasn't McCorkle. The tall man turned and there stood Buckskin Frank Leslie. Both men drew. Both men fired. Both men died. Morgan blinked and cursed under his breath as the end of his cigarette reached his finger.

He walked back over and lay down, his arms up and his hands underneath his head. Is that the way it will end? He and Jace Kileen both dead? Tom Horn snored again. Morgan closed his eyes. He saw his father's face . . . looking up at him . . . smiling. The red spot on his chest growing bigger with each breath. Who would hold Morgan's head? Was he like Harvey Logan . . . and Kileen the old time shootist? Morgan dozed.

The rattling of the coffee pot brought Morgan from the deepest sleep he'd experienced in weeks. Sunshine streamed through the windows of the sheriff's office. He caught the movement of someone . . . Petie.

"What the hell time is it?"

"Well now . . . mornin' Mister Morgan. Seemed to me, there fer a spell, you just might sleep out the day."

Morgan sat up and then got to his feet. He was irritated. "Damn it, old man, what time is it?"

"Jist past ten."

"*Ten!*" Morgan looked around. Petie walked up, smiled and handed him a cup of coffee. "Where's Horn?"

"Asked me to give you this." Morgan took the slip of paper. He sat down at the desk, took a short sip of coffee, set the cup down and unfolded the paper.

> One of Belle's gals come by . . . said two fellas left early riding to Ketchum. She heard they was riding to kill Marshal Rawlings. May be they just want to split us. It worked. Can't let Seth get it. I'll dog them two and git back soon as I can. Watch yourself, son.
>
> Tom Horn

"Goddamn fool," Morgan said. "They'll be laying

for him not five miles out.''

"That there is about what he said.'' Morgan
looked up. Petie was smiling. "Mister Horn . . . he's
been around a long time . . . he got worse than the
likes o' those two. I wouldn't worry none 'bout him,
Mister Morgan. It's you what's gonna face down
Jace Kileen.''

Morgan checked the load in the Smith and
Wesson, loaded the sixth chamber and strapped on
the rig. He sat back down and sipped his coffee.
Outside, the bustle of Boise seemed undisturbed by
the presence of the participants of the drama. No
law existed now but most citizens didn't even know
it. The newspaper was afraid to send a reporter to
the Four Queens. Morgan knew there would be no
posse formed up in Boise. No vigilantes would ride
in and shoot it out at the saloon. Doubtless, his
death or that of Kileen's would go unnoticed.

Morgan finished his coffee, slipped on his coat,
smiled at Petie and walked out. It was a block and a
half to the Four Queens. Down Rose Hill from
Shoshone, past the railroad depot and then right
onto Vista. "Mister Morgan . . . Mister Morgan . . .
you forgot somethin'.'' Morgan turned. Petie held
up his hand and Morgan saw the glint of the sun on
the tin star.

"Shit,'' Morgan muttered. He walked back,
nodded at Petie, took the badge and pinned it to his
coat. Then he turned back and walked to the corner.
He stayed to the sidewalks but noticed that the
number of people on the streets had diminished. He
reached Vista, paused and glanced toward the
railroad depot. He saw a little knot of men by the
corner of the building. They saw him. They shuffled,
nervous. One of them pointed at Morgan. They
knew. He walked to the middle of the street, eyed

each building carefully and then turned toward the saloon.

Up in Belle Moran's office, the door opened. A nervous little man poked his head inside. Jace Kileen was leaning against the wall, arms folded across his chest. Senator Tom Yeager was seated at the desk.

"What is it, Rollins?"

"He's coming sir . . . not the old one . . . the young one."

"Thank you," Yeager said. He swallowed. The door closed. He looked at Kileen. Kileen smiled. "Well?"

"Cody will handle him."

"And if he doesn't?"

"Then I'll know he's better than I figure he is."

"And you sent the others off on a wild goose chase after some damned old lawman."

"Seth Rawlings is a better man than you've ever seen, Senator."

"That's not the point. What if this Morgan gets by you?"

"He won't."

"I'm not in a position to risk that. . . am I?"

"You fuck with me," Kileen said icily, "and I'll live long enough to kill you Yeager . . . mark me on that."

"I . . . I don't see how . . . how *everything* could have gone wrong."

"Real easy. You had all the wrong men thinking for you."

"Are you at least going downstairs . . . just in case?" Kileen smiled . . . then he nodded. When he reached the door, Yeager said, "Get him, Kileen. Make sure you get him."

"Sure, Yeager, you just relax." Kileen walked out

and Tom Yeager wiped his brow, walked to the window and peered out. Seeing nothing at the back of the saloon, he disappeared into the sleeping quarters.

Downstairs, the kid named Cody shoved a big tin plate away from him, took two swallows of coffee and sucked some bacon out of his front teeth. He looked up and saw Jace Kileen.

"Mornin' Jace."

"Morgan's outside."

"Yeah . . . I know." Cody grinned, hefted the twin Colts and let them slip back into their holsters. Then he hefted his right leg onto a chair and tied down his holster. He repeated the process on the left side.

"I've heard he's good, Cody. Son of old Frank Leslie."

"I heard o' Leslie. Harvey Logan took him out." Cody grinned. "Now there was a fast gun . . . Kid Curry."

"Leslie killed him . . . he didn't gain much."

"Well I ain't Logan . . . an' this gunny ain't his daddy." A man at the front door backed off, swallowing. He turned and looked at Kileen and the kid called Cody. "Out front . . . that's Lee Morgan."

Cody doffed his hat. "See you in a minute Jace. Buy you the first drink o' the day." Cody walked to the front door, opened it and walked out. He closed it behind him and then turned. Lee Morgan stood in the middle of the street. The little knot of men from the depot had moved to about half a block away. Another group had formed in the other direction. All had come to see a man die. Morgan doubted that it made any difference to them which man it was.

"Well now . . . we got ourselves some new law in Boise. You takin' up for Tate Bosley are you?"

"Deputy Territorial Marshal," Morgan said,

"deputy to Seth Rawlings."

"That right. My name's Cody. That's my *first* name. Only one you'll be needin' to know."

"You're under arrest," Morgan said. At the same time, the hem of the sheepskin coat went back. Cody made his move. Both hands, both Colts . . . three shots. The first two dug into the snow and the dirt on Vista Street. They were just beneath the toes of Morgan's boots. The third shot, out of the right hand gun, went high and wild. It was fired by the reflex action of a dead man. Morgan fired only one shot. It penetrated Cody's left eye, tore it from the socket and drove it, along with a fragment of nose bone, into Cody's brain.

Cody's body smashed into the saloon's door. His left elbow went through the window. The signal from the opposite side of his brain sent the message that caused him to fire the third shot. He was already dead. His body hung on the door a moment, stiffened, teetered precariously as though seeking equilibrium and then fell foward.

A man at the window stepped back. "I never seen nobody draw that fast . . . not nobody. Not even from the old days." The man turned and looked right straight at Jace Kileen. "He kil't Cody with one shot." Jace reached up and wiped his mouth. He turned and walked to the bar.

"What'll you have, Mister Kileen?"

"Tennessee mash," Kileen replied. Then he turned and faced the door.

Tom Horn's mount pulled up short on a hillock about twenty miles outside of Boise. He dropped his head and pawed. He raised his head and snorted. A shot rang out and the animal staggered, whinnied and dropped in its tracks. The horse kicked its legs and four more shots rang out. The animal was still. So was its rider. All four shots had hit home.

Two men emerged from a stand of trees on either side of the rise. They met at the spiny summit, spoke to each other in low tones and then walked toward their victims. Once there, they split up. One man knelt by the animal. It was dead. The other by the man.

"Jeezus Christ . . . he . . . he's *dead!*" The man leaped to his feet.

" 'Course he's dead you goddam fool," the other man said, standing up now.

"Oh shit . . . oh billy shit." The man who'd knelt by the horse's rider turned white, his eyes grew big and he started turning . . . 'round and 'round. "He was *already* dead." He pointed to the man on the horse. "It's Eddie . . . Eddie Hargrove. Oh shit . . . Billy shit." The Creedmoor barked. The frightened man's body was slammed into the snow, face first, with the force equivalent to having been hit in the head with a sledge hammer. He never moved again.

The second man stood . . . unbelieving . . . frozen . . . numb with the realization he was about to die. He turned on his heel . . . his brain's message finally reaching reluctant legs. The Creedmoor barked a second time and the whole back of the man's head disappeared behind a shock of thick, brown hair and a black, flat crowned hat.

Tom Horn had experienced the horse killers before —up near Gunsmoke Gorge. He'd risen early, listened to the girl's report and then rounded up his gear and borrowed a horse from the livery. Tom then rode to the mortuary and, at gunpoint, found himself a cadaver. An hour in the morning air gave the body all the stiffness required for it to sit a horse. Horn dogged the two men's trail until it split.

Then, he dismounted, replaced himself with the body of Eddie Hargrove, dropped the reins on the horse and slapped its thighs. The horse moved off along the ridge almost at a walk. Creedmoor in hand, Tom Horn took to the trees, finally positioned himself at the split in the trail and waited.

Tom had no trouble rounding up the men's horses. He tied both of them to one horse, draped Eddie's body over the back of his own, mounted up and headed back to Boise.

The saloon door opened and Cody's body came through it. Morgan stepped in behind, quickly surveyed the scene and then looked straight at Jace Kileen.

"I think he belongs to you," Morgan said.

"I knew him." Several men in the bar moved back to the far wall. Morgan's eyes remained riveted on those of Jace Kileen. "You're pretty good."

"You're under arrest, Kileen."

"You're not *that* good." Kileen drank a shot of whiskey, wiped his mouth and stepped away from the bar. He smiled. "It's really not me you want anyway, is it, Morgan?"

"You'll do, Kileen . . . for starters . . . for Ephram Culpepper." Kileen smirked. "The old preacher man. Always thought he could take me. We were trail compadres once—a long time back."

"You're a talker Kileen . . . talk 'til you buffalo a man."

"Tomorrow, Morgan . . . right here." Kileen nodded toward a table. "I'll have the man you *really* want right over there . . . so he can watch. Take me . . . and he's yours."

"I can have him right now."

"No, you can't. I've got a man upstairs with a

shotgun on him. Any noise down here and he dies."

Morgan reacted for the first time to something Kileen had said. Kileen smiled. Morgan said, "What's the difference Kileen? Today or tomorrow it'll end the same way."

"True . . . but I sent two men out to fetch back Seth Rawlings. You see . . . he's the man I want. You're in my way getting to him just like I'm in yours getting to who you want. Tomorrow . . . Rawlings will be here . . . alive. After I've settled him, you'll have your chance."

"You sure about those men you sent out . . . sure they'll make it?"

"Why shouldn't they?"

"Because Tom Horn found out about them. He rode out of Boise less than an hour behind them, Kileen. Now surely . . . I don't have to tell *you* about Tom Horn." Now it was Morgan's turn to get a reaction. He did. Kileen's face paled. Morgan had a little edge. "I'll make you a deal," he said, smiling, "if Horn rides back in anytime today, I'll be back for you. If not . . . we'll do it your way . . . Seth Rawlings and all."

"Done," Kileen said. His voice did not carry in its tone his earlier conviction. Morgan backed to the door, stepped over Cody's body and outside. "I'll enjoy taking you, Morgan. You might offer some serious competition." Morgan didn't reply.

Judge Isaac Barr had risen early that same morning as well. He had been staying at the home of Ada county prosecutor, James Bidwell. It was located in nearby Nampa, Idaho. Bidwell was more than a little cornered with his old friend's state of mind.

"Judge . . . for God's sake . . . you can't ride into

Boise until I hear from Tate Bosley. We don't know the situation."

"Jim," Isaac Barr said, putting his hand on Bidwell's shoulder, "are you going to stop me at gunpoint?"

"For God's sake . . . no!"

"Then you can't stop me at all. You know it and you know why."

"This man Morgan . . . and Tom Horn . . . Tate and his men . . . they can handle things."

"You were supposed to hear something yesterday from your assistant. You didn't. Something is wrong."

"Judge . . . he could have gotten tied up with anything. At least give it one more day."

"No Jim . . . I'm sorry . . . I can't. I just simply can't."

Judge Bar ate a small breakfast, finished dressing and asked the stable boy to ready his horse.

"At least take my buggy."

"I'll ride in. I want to see Yeager's face just once before I die. I want to see how he must look . . . how he must *feel* about the man he's become . . . and what he . . . what he's done to me . . . and mine."

"My God, man! Stop torturing yourself. You don't know for sure about Morgana. No one has seen her. No one has heard anything."

"Goodbye, Jim, and thank you," Barr said. Jim Bidwell watched Isaac Barr ride away. Immediately, he dressed, readied his buggy and set off behind the judge.

Lee Morgan sat in the sheriff's office and cleaned his weapons . . . twice. His mind kept going back to the kid named Cody. Had Morgan drawn as fast as he could have? He shook the thought away. But it came back. If he had, Cody had come close. Surely Jace Kileen was faster . . . much faster. If Morgan hadn't used all his speed how much more could he call upon? He didn't know.

Buckskin Frank Leslie told him once that the difference between living and dying in a gun fight was often no more than to be willing to die if that's what had to be done. Most men, he'd said, weren't willing. Sometimes they recognized it only at the last moment. A split second of time in their lives when their minds ask the silent question. During that moment—that ever so minute speck of time—their opponent had the edge.

The door opened and Morgan looked up. "Mornin'," Tom Horn said. Morgan poured the coffee, Tom did the talking. Morgan then told Tom what had happened over at the Four Queens.

"Kileen feels pretty safe right now," Tom finally said. "If he's to be taken, now's the time."

"If I don't make it," Morgan said, his voice even in tone and almost passive about the subject, "bury me next to my dad. That cemetery—at least the rights to use it—that stayed with me when the Bit was sold." Horn just nodded. He loaded the Parker and put his coat and hat back on. Morgan frowned.

"I'll back you against anybody else that might figger to make a name fer themselves."

"I lose," Morgan said, grimly, "Kileen might just kill you too."

"Doubt that. Kileen is an old timer. Got a code. Like your daddy had. Knows he could kill me face-to-face an' he don't fight no other way. He might send somebody after me . . . like them two this mornin' . . . but he won't do it."

"What if you're wrong Tom?"

Horn grinned. "Got another hold up there by your

daddy?'' Morgan shook his head and walked out. Horn fell in beside him.

A block and a half away, the door at the Four Queens opened. A man rushed inside, looked around and then hollered, "Jace Kileen in here?"

"Here," Kileen replied. He was in a far corner, seated with three other men. They were playing poker. Kileen stood up.

"That fella Morgan is on his way over," the man paused, drew a deep breath and then added, "Tom Horn is with him." No one really saw the expression on Kileen's face but a moment later, he turned to the men at the table and smiled.

"Sorry, gents, you'll have to excuse me for a few minutes." Out on the street, the word spread even faster than it had earlier. In part, it had come from the undertaker. Tom Horn had dropped off three bodies, apologized for his earlier theft and payed for all the preparations. By the time he and Morgan turned onto Vista, quite a crowd had gathered.

Uptairs in the saloon, Tom Yeager was in the living quarters. There was a window which overlooked Vista Street. He heard the commotion, pulled the curtain back, looked out and sucked in several short gasps of air. He hurried out of the room, through the office, into the hallway and stopped at the head of the stairs. Jace Kileen was just opening the front door.

"Kileen!" Jace paused for a second but nothing more. He said nothing and he did not acknowledge Yeager's single spoken word. He walked out and into the street. Tom Horn and Lee Morgan were about seventy-five yards away. Horn stopped. Morgan did not. Horn walked to the side of the street, scanning the nearby buildings for signs of any back-up men. He saw nothing but cocked both barrels on the Parker.

Morgan had slowed his pace just a little . . . but he was still walking. 65 yards . . . 60 . . . 55 . . . 45. Jace Kileen moved his coat tail and exposed the butt of his pistol. A faint smile rippled across his thin lips. Still Morgan came at him. 30 yards . . . 25 . . . 20. Kileen spread his feet slightly and his shoulders visibly sagged as the tension flowed from them.

"Your round," Kileen said. Now, he was smiling . . . a broad, almost beaming smile. Lee Morgan said nothing and never broke his pace. 15 yards . . . 14 . . . 13 . . . Jace Kileen's brow wrinkled ever so slightly. 12 yards . . . 11 . . . 10 . . . Kileen said, "Morgan . . ."

There were twenty-seven witnesses to what occurred. A dozen of them were in positions to see every detail of the scenario. Some would speak of it for years. None would ever forget.

At eight yards distance . . . 24 feet . . . Jace Kileen's mouth opened. He faced more men in his life than Lee Morgan probably knew. He'd never experienced a man who didn't stop . . . who wouldn't stop . . . who ignored everything except the barest necessity of life . . . breathing! Kileen recognized an iron will . . . a steel-nerved determination to do what no one would believe *could* be done.

This recognition required thought . . . emotional action and a pause for reaction. Given a lesser man than Lee Morgan . . . Kileen's skill and speed with a gun would have offset the lost time. Kileen suddenly realized that Lee Moran *wasn't* a lesser man. Kileen's hand moved with the same smooth flow, the same practiced style that it had for twenty-five years. He was no slower—no less accurate—he was just a split second later in starting.

Morgan's little Smith and Wesson cracked loudly —*twice!* The first shot already fading by the time the second was fired. Between them, almost unheard, Jace Kileen fired. Kileen's bullet traced an angled trajectory and cut a groove of flesh from the upper inside of Lee Morgan's left thigh. Kileen lived long enough to realize it.

Morgan's first shot shattered Kileen's sternum. Bone fragments pierced his right lung and severed a number of blood vessels. Morgan's second shot was a few inches off target. He hadn't allowed for the backward movement of Kileen's body. The bullet entered Kileen's jaw just beneath his chin. It traveled upward, pierced the back of his tongue, passed through his head and exited at the base of his skull.

Lee Morgan was still walking. He did not stop until he was standing over Jace Kileen's motionless form. In his mind's eye, Morgan saw the face of Kid Curry . . . Harvey Logan . . . dead at the hand of Buckskin Frank Leslie. A moment later, Morgan saw Kileen's face. His eyes fluttered, his right leg twitched and the crotch of his denim showed a dark blue, wet spot which continued to spread.

Morgan holstered the S and W, turned, winced in pain and staggered slightly as he took a step. Tom Horn moved toward him at a trot. Lee regained his balance and smiled . . . moving off toward the door of the Four Queens. He could hear disjointed words . . . parts of sentences . . . bits of comment.

"See that . . . fastest man alive . . . Kileen was scared . . . Morgan . . . Frank Leslie . . . Jeezus that was somethin' . . . never believe . . ." Morgan reached the door, Tom Horn reached Morgan.

"You're good boy . . . I believe you're better'n ol' Leslie." Morgan looked at Tom Horn and a half smile crossed his lips. He said, "I was better than Jace Kileen and that's all the better I had to be."

The two men went inside after Tom Horn ordered one of the bystanders to fetch the doctor.

Upstairs, U.S. Senator Thomas Yeager poured himself a straight shot of whiskey, downed it with a shaky hand and slumped into a chair. He sat staring at the wall. Somewhere behind him a door opened and closed. He didn't hear it.

15

Just forty-eight hours before the gun fight that would keep all of Boise talking for years, U.S. Marshal Seth Rawlings had crawled into a buggy seat. Most who were nearby were protesting loudly about his action. He ignored them as did his companion, Belle Moran. A few minutes later they set out for Boise.

"You know," Belle said, "I agree with those folks. I don't think you should make this trip."

Seth looked at her and smiled. "But you understand . . . don't you?"

She nodded. "How long you known Morgan?"

"More years than I'll admit to," she replied.

"He's not that damned old." Seth realized, too late, what his observation inferred. He grinned at his lack of tact.

"I'll let that pass," Belle said.

"You know his daddy?"

"Uh huh. God . . . there *was* a man."

"A gun fighter."

"A *man* first." Belle glanced over at the aging marshal. "His kind were needed back then. You were around. You know it."

"He walked on both sides of the law. Don't make him any less guilty than a man who never walks but the wrong side."

"You don't believe that tripe, Seth. That's putting Buckskin Frank Leslie in the same box with Jace Kileen."

"Wasn't he?"

"Hell *no*. Kileen does what he wants to do. Frank," she smiled, wistfully, as she thought about him, "he did what he *had* to do."

"Mebbe."

"You were lawin' even then, Seth. How's come you never went after him if you thought he was so damned bad?"

"Never knew it was him . . . not fer sure anyways . . . not 'til Harvey Logan rode in an' killed him. Then . . . well, it all come out."

"An' his son? When did you meet him?"

"Same time. Greenhorn kid . . . scared . . . madder'n a swatted hornet and frustrated as to what to do about it."

Belle frowned. "Is he good enough to take Kileen?"

"Yeah," Seth replied without hesitation. "He's good enough." He looked into Belle's eyes now and added, "But I'm not sure *he* knows it."

"And you . . . are *you* good enough?"

"No. Never was. Mebbe that's one reason I didn't go after old Frank Leslie. Mebbe I knew even then I wasn't the same cut."

"I've heard you're one of the best."

Seth smiled. "One . . . that there's the key word . . . one o' the best. I don't use a gun the same way those men do . . . or did. Makes me vulnerable."

"You knew a lot of them didn't you . . . the old timers?"

"Yeah . . . most. Hickok . . . Earp . . . Masterson. Doc Holliday too." Belle smiled and raised her eyebrows. "I heard he was about the handsomest devil around."

"I s'pose any woman would have thought so."

"Who was the best . . . the very, very best?"

"Don't think I can answer that one Belle. Don't think *anybody* can. I reckon four come to muh mind first if'n I think back. Hickok . . . Holliday . . . Frank Leslie and J.W. Hardin."

"But you can't pick the best huh?"

"Nope. Coolest heads were on Holliday's shoulders . . . an' Leslie's. Flat out speed? Prob'ly Johnny Hardin. Accuracy? No doubt about that . . . James Butler Hickok."

"And what about Lee Morgan?"

"He's got a ways to go yet . . . gotta live more years."

"Kileen?"

"Couldn't have taken a single one o' them I jist mentioned. Neither could Morgan, but he's got the coolest head if he'll just use it."

"I saw Hardin once," Belle said, "down in Abilene. I was just startin' out. Fella name of Deke Brokaw an' a couple o' friends o' his decided mister Hardin would stake their reputations.

"I remember hearin' 'bout a Brokaw."

"Hmm. He was real good. Called Mister Hardin out while he was standin' at the bar. Hell, Hardin had a glass o' whiskey in his left hand when Brokaw drew. Hardin killed him an' never spilled a drop. Then he drank the whiskey, walked to the door, turned back around an' called out the other two. They were at opposite sides o' the room. He killed 'em both. One shot each. Then he just walked out."

"I'd like to git Lee Morgan to deputy for me—permanent." Belle looked surprised. The statement had come from nowhere. Seth was looking at Belle. "Would you help me?"

"Hell, he won't listen to me."

"He might. He come back to Idaho to stay. Got no ranch now. He'll need somethin'."

"Lee's a drifter an' he's got no use for lawmen."

"He'll end up on some street, suckin' air through a hole in his chest. They'll mount 'im on a plank board an' charge ten cents to git a look see."

"I'll talk to him Seth. I'll try."

Morgan walked back to the sheriff's office and changed his britches. He reloaded his pistol and then went back to the Four Queens. He'd left Tom Horn there to make certain no one left. Tom recruited a youngster to keep an eye on the back way out.

"Your man's upstairs," Tom said.

"Do me one more favor." Horn looked quizzical. "Walk over to the newspaper office and bring back a reporter. They'll come if you ask 'em to. I want to tell the story. All of it. I want it out before that Senator is brought down."

"No need," Horn said. "Soon as they heard Jace Kileen was dead, their man came runnin'. Howard Bracken is 'is name." Horn pointed. "That's him . . . fella at the end o' the bar. He owns the newspaper."

"Mister Morgan," Bracken said, smiling and extending his hand. Morgan shook it. "I'd hoped to get a chance to talk to you. I've heard some disturbing stories."

"About Idaho's real honest to God Senator?"

"Yes. I've known Tom Yeager a long time. Like to think I helped him get elected."

"Nothing wrong with that . . . then."

"Can you prove what you're claiming?"

"He can."

"Sure," Bracken agreed, laughing, "if he'll admit

it."

"He'll admit it."

"At the point of a gun? He's no Jace Kileen and I've not heard or seen anything to prove a connection between the two."

"Your senator friend was supposed to have left town. He didn't."

"So I gather, but that doesn't prove much except that he's still in Boise . . . upstairs."

"Why don't I tell you what I know. Then we'll see about proving it."

"Shall we?" Bracken said, pointing to a table. Morgan nodded.

Howard Bracken listened, questioned and wrote for more than two hours. He heard about the marauders, the professional hired on both sides, the fortress at Gunsmoke Gorge and the trail which had led, finally, to this meeting.

"I don't think you conjured all this up, Mister Morgan," Bracken finally said, "but I'm wondering if a deputy an' a kind of unofficial one at that, can carry on from here?"

"I can answer that question, Howard." Morgan and Bracken both jerked their heads around and saw Seth Rawlings at the door. Beside him was Belle Moran. "I'd have been here sooner but we stopped off at the courthouse." Seth handed Bracken a paper. Bracken looked at it. It was a warrant for the arrest of Senator Thomas Yeager.

Morgan looked down at Seth's leg. Blood was soaking through his britches. "Get the doc back," Morgan said to Tom.

"I'll live."

"Yeah you will . . . if I have to shoot you so the doc can fix you up again." Seth laughed for the first time in weeks. "I want the arrest."

"And I want you permanent," Seth said. Belle looked shocked. "I'll do my own dirty work," Seth said to her. He looked back at Morgan.

"No deal."

"You're a hard-headed son-of-a-bitch, Morgan."

"No offense in this refusal," Morgan said. "There's too many things to remember in Idaho for me. I might get to thinking about them and get myself shot . . . or worse . . . somebody else."

Seth winced . . . looked at his leg and then sat down. He looked up. "I can't argue the logic in that, damn it! As for the arrest, it's yours. You sure as hell earned it."

"I sent a boy for the doc," Tom said.

"Will you back me upstairs . . . just in case?" Horn nodded.

"Ladies and Gentlemen . . . please . . . your attention . . . please." Everyone turned to the sound of the voice. There, at the top of the stairs, was Senator Thomas Yeager. His arms were up in the air. Some of the crowd gasped. They knew only what they had already heard—that Yeager had left Boise.

"A terrible, terrible thing happened this morning in Boise. Something that civilization can no longer tolerate. A shooting in the street. Gunplay reminiscent of a quarter century ago." He coughed and cleared his throat.

He put his arms down. "I came to Boise to personally put an end to the marauding raids on helpless ranchers . . . to restore law and order to this great state. Instead, I found myself the participant . . . and the victim . . . of a vile intrigue which reaches to the very seat of our nation's power."

Seth, Morgan, Horn and many others moved nearer the steps. At the very forefront was Howard Bracken. Moments later, a photographer appeared and pushed his way through the crowd.

"Some of my own aides were involved in these criminal acts. I found myself fearful . . . desperate. I grasped at even the most feeble straws of credibility. As a result, I fell under the influence of evil men . . . men like Jace Kileen . . . a man named Brock and my own, personal aide, Ted Peabody."

The crowd gasped. Others from the street had pushed their way in. Yeager was in his element and he was *winning*.

Morgan started to go upstairs. A firm hand gripped his arm. He turned. It was Seth. "Not here," he said, softly, "and not now."

"The bastard is lying."

"But he's doing it on his ground," Seth said, "and if you face him now he'll be a hell of a lot tougher opponent than Jace Kileen was. He's got a power that beats hell out of a Colt's revolver." Morgan studied Seth's face. Somehow, he wasn't exactly certain why, Morgan knew Seth was right.

"Even as these events were unfolding—tragic as it may be—I had to allow them. Men like Mister Morgan . . . our fine Sheriff, Tate Bosley and his deputies . . . and U.S. Marshal Seth Rawlings bought me the most precious commodity a politician can have . . . *time*. Now with these heroic deeds and the law quietly at work behind the scenes, justice has prevailed. Ladies and gentleman . . . law and order have won. Idaho is at peace with itself."

A cheer went up, along with hats. Guns were fired into the ceiling and as the word spread to the outside, the scene became a melee of joy. When order was restored, allowed simply to run its course, the crowd finally settled. Senator Yeager, smiling broadly, concluded.

"Formal tributes and a proper ceremony will be

announced. For now, I ask you to return to your homes and allow me to return to Washington. There, I will formalize the report and see to it that formal charges are leveled at those still free who raised their hands against our sovereign state."

Amid the din of more cheering, Senator Thomas Yeager retreated to Belle Moran's office. In a few moments, he would walk down the stairs, through the crowd, down to the train depot and depart Boise. He would do so with the blessing and protection of its citizens. Anyone moving against him would be dealt with harshly.

"Get out that damned warrant," Morgan said.

"It's not worth the paper it's written on . . . not now it isn't."

Howard Bracken overheard the comment and turned to Lee Morgan. "The good marshal is right, Mister Morgan. Even if every word you told me this morning is gospel."

"You doubting it now?"

"I never doubted anything," Bracken said. He pointed upstairs. "I don't doubt what he said. In neither case does that imply that I believe it. I've heard it. Now, I'll do my best to sort it out . . . to squeeze from the fruit . . . the juice of the truth."

Morgan said, "You've got a fine way with words, Mister Bracken, but you're one gullible son-of-a-bitch." In an instant, Morgan had grabbed the arrest warrant from Seth's hand and gained the top of the stairs. He drew the S and W, fired one shot at the ceiling and then holstered the gun.

"Some of you know me by name . . . some don't know me at all and I'd guess that most don't give a damn either way . . . but now you'll listen to *me*." He held up the warrant. "This paper is a warrant issued by your own local, lovable, Judge Tyrone P. Riddle.

It's a warrant for the arrest of the man you just heard . . . of Senator Thomas Yeager.'' Morgan paused. The reaction was one of stunned silence but he did have the crowd's attention. Howard Bracken was quietly impressed.

"I don't believe," Morgan continued, "that the judge would have issued this warrant without cause. It's my job to serve it and make the arrest." He heard some moans and grumbling. He waited. "We fought a war a few years back over this very thing . . . the right of a state to conduct its own business. Granted, there were men who abused the right . . . treated fellow human beings badly . . . but the issue when settled, still restored the right of local law."

"What's any o' that got to do with Yeager? He's no crook."

"Maybe he's not," Morgan snapped, "but if he's not . . . let me prove it in Idaho . . . not Washington. Let the law . . . your law . . . work. Hell, it wasn't Washington where these bastards burned out ranches, it was Idaho. Is he above it because he's a senator? Am I . . . or Seth Rawlilngs here . . . are we above the law because we wear badges?"

The crowd mumbled, there were isolated shouts of "No!" and then a ripple of support which turned into a wave of cheering. One man then shouted above the din.

"My ranch was burned out . . . my family killed. Let Yeager answer *that* in court . . . here . . . do it here in Idaho."

"Yeah . . take him in, deputy. Let's find out."

Morgan nodded and walked to the bottom of the stairs. Howard Bracken smiled. "You're an eloquent son-of-a-bitch," he said. "I didn't think you had it in you."

"I probably spoke out of turn," Morgan said. He turned to Seth. "Well?" He was holding out the warrant. Seth looked at it, at Morgan, at Howard Bracken and then back to Morgan.

"Serve the goddam thing," Seth said.

Morgan turned and started up the stairway. Half way up, he stopped. He looked down a moment and then he turned back to the crowd. "One more thing," he shouted. The crowd turned silent. "Tom Yeager will remain innocent of anything until the law finds him guilty. Some of you will be asked to judge him. Do it from the evidence . . . not from anything anybody . . . him or I . . . have said."

"What's he charged with, Deputy?"

"The warrant says fraud, abuse of the power of an official office and conspiracy to commit murder. I'll arrest him and I'll stand against any man who tries to interfere with the legal procedure after that." No one, particularly those who witnessed Morgan's confrontations with Cody and Jace Kileen, cared to argue with him. He turned back.

The shot seemed very loud. So did the woman's scream. A door slammed shut. Morgan cleared the rest of the stairs two at a time. He rushed to Belle's office . . . gun drawn. He stepped back and kicked the door open, pistol at the ready. There was nothing but silence. He entered the room.

U. S. Senator Thomas Yeager was seated at Belle's desk. His left arm was on the desk and his head rested on it. His right arm dangled at his side. There was a thud behind the desk. Morgan walked over.

"God damn," Morgan exclaimed. The pistol, a tiny wisp of smoke still curling up from its barrel, had fallen from his hand. A steady stream of blood flowed from Yeager's right temple. He turned and walked out of the office . . . checking in both directions in the corridor. He saw nothing. He heard nothing. He wondered about the door he'd heard slam. He walked back to the stairway.

"Morgan! What happened up there?" Bracken asked. Seth Rawlings seemed to know. Tom Horn was helping Seth start up the stairs.

"Yeager is dead. He put a bullet in his head or so it appears." The crowd chattered but there was no outburst. Seth and Tom were about half way up when Seth stopped dead in his tracks. He was looking up and to his left. Tom followed his line of vision. Morgan looked puzzled.

"You killed him . . . you *bastard!* You drove him to it!" Morgan wheeled but he didn't draw his gun. The voice belonged to a woman. He saw the shotgun first, both barrels levelled at his chest . . . ten feet away. Holding it was Morgana Barr.

"Morgana . . . don't!" She glanced at Seth, spat in his direction and raised the shotgun. Another shot echoed through the corridor of the Four Queens saloon. It came from the darkness just behind Morgana Barr. Her eyes grew big . . . her mouth dropped open and the shotgun dropped from her hands and clattered to the floor. She staggered and then fell, face forward.

Out of the shadows . . . dazed by what he had seen and what he had done was Judge Isaac Barr. He dropped to his knees beside the body of his dead daughter. The daughter he'd just killed. He was sobbing. No one else moved. The old judge struggled back to his feet and slowly, very slowly, raised the pistol.

"Isaac . . . Jeezus . . . no!" Morgan lurched forward. Judge Barr looked down and then up. He turned the gun end for end and handed it to Morgan.

"It's over," he said softly. "It's finally all over."

In fact, it wasn't over.

16

Two trials were held in the district court in Ada county Idaho that year. The first was held *in Absentia*. The accused was U.S. Senator Thomas Yeager. At the conclusion of the more than two months of testimony, much of it from participants such as Tom Horn, Lee Morgan and the rancher's association members, Yeager was found guilty on all charges. Two weeks later, Judge Isaac Barr was brought to trail on charges of murder in the death of his daughter.

The jury heard two weeks worth of testimony . . . much of it from the judge himself. The juror's were finally sequestered to ponder the judge's fate on the 22nd day of December at just past noon.

"What do you think, Seth?" Morgan asked after they got back to the sheriff's office.

"Can't do much more than find him guilty. Hell, he shot her in front of a whole goddamn room full of witnesses . . . and admitted it to boot."

"Did he ride in with that in mind?"

"Nope. Manslaughter . . . that's what they'll find." Seth looked at Tom Horn.

Tom nodded and said, "Sentence him to jail an' then suspend it."

"I hope you're right," Morgan said.

"They will . . . no doubt. The one thing about this

194

country that I got great faith in is the legal system. Seen it work good for near forty years. It's slow but it works."

"You've never seen it fail?" Morgan asked Tom.

"Nope. Leastways not where a man's life is dependin' on it. Never knowed a man hanged that didn't deserve to be—by the law I mean."

"There's always a first time."

"You're a cynical bastard," Tom said, grinning. "I s'pose it could happen but I don't think I'll ever see it. Mostly men are fair. They try. Anyways," Horn added thoughtfully, "even if a mistake was made . . . even if a man died . . . the system shouldn't be thrown out. It serves more right than wrong. That's the best anybody can hope for."

"He's had enough punishment anyway," Seth said. He hit on his leg, sore and still stiff from the gunshot wound. He sat down. "I don't know if I could have done what he did. Killed his own flesh and blood. God! What a decision to make!"

"Yeah," Morgan said, "I know. I made it once. I went looking for my father. I hated him then. I wanted him dead. I had my chance. I figure he'd have killed me too . . . mostly out of reflex action . . . but I couldn't do it."

"I guess old Isaac figured she'd done enough. He'd suspected for a long time . . . wasn't certain of it 'til he sent you that note to back off."

"Yeah . . . he figured she'd backshoot me the first chance she got."

"That was one I couldn't figure," Tom said. "How's come you s'pose she didn't?"

"The only thing I could ever make of it was that she thought I'd do more good for the marauders than bad. I had all the right contacts with all the right people . . . Killerman . . . Strada . . . her daddy .

. . even the law. Besides, she knew about Brock and Cody and Jessup."

"An' Jace Kileen." Seth shook his head. "That's one I regret missin'." He looked up at Morgan. "You give anymore thought to stayin' on?"

"Yeah."

"And?"

"No good. I told you why. It still holds."

"What then? And where?" Lee Morgan shrugged. The door opened. Seth's new deputy, George Tyson, stuck his head in the door.

"Jury's in."

"Gentlemen," Judge Riddle said, "have you reached a verdict?"

"We have, Your Honor. We find Judge Isaac Barr guilty of the second charge of manslaughter."

Judge Riddle thanked the jury, set sentencing for two weeks hence and closed the case.

Back in his cell at the county jail, Isaac Barr asked Seth, Lee Morgan and Tom Horn to visit him. They complied.

"I'm hoping that you, Morgan, and you Mister Horn, will stay in Boise for two more weeks until I'm sentenced."

"If you'd like, Judge. I'll stay," Morgan said.

Tom Horn grinned. "Seems I can't rightly recollect a passle o' invites from anybody wantin' to see me lately. I'll stick around."

"Good. Then the lot of you are invited to the Rocky Barr on that day. We've some celebrating to do and some settling of accounts." All three men looked somewhat stunned. Judge Barr smiled. "If I were on the bench, I'd give myself a suspended sentence . . . with probation time."

Judge Barr, quite out of character, swelled

himself up and said, tongue-in-cheek, "And I am, by Godfrey, a better judge than old Riddle." They all laughed.

Seth released Isaac from his cell each evening and they sat and played checkers. On one such an evening, three days before Isaac was to be sentenced, the door opened. Riley Preston, Ada county's Democratic chairman, walked in.

"Gentlemen . . . good evening," Isaac smiled, wryly. Seth frowned. "May I," Preston said, gesturing toward a chair. Seth nodded, Riley sat. "We have an unexpired Senate term to fill . . . about eighteen months worth. We've been wrestling with the problem but during the past three weeks . . . thanks to Isaac Barr's suggestion . . . we've taken a poll and reached a solution."

"Well . . . I'm proud of you," Seth said, dryly, "but what brings you here?"

"The voters we polled picked from five names on a list. One man got more votes than all the rest combined. Now Isaac here . . . he couldn't be considered of course." Seth frowned and looked at both men. They were looking back . . . and both smiling. "You won, Marshal."

"Bull dung!"

"See for yourself." Preston handed Seth the day's issue of the Boise paper. The news report confirmed what Preston had just revealed.

"I'm no goddam politician. I'm a lawman."

"With that leg," Isaac said, pointing. "Besides, you're too old to ride all over the circuit. George Tyson isn't. He's been a good deputy and he'd make a good territorial marshal."

"Well . . . I won't do it," Seth said. "Too damned old or not." Preston got to his feet, slapped Seth on the shoulder and said, "Fair enough, Marshal. Now

all you have to do is tell the folks you've turned
them down and then ask them to vote for you again
for the sheriff's job you wanted."

"You're blackmailing me!"

"That's a fair assessment, Marshal . . . only it's all
very legal." Preston waved his goodbye as he went
out.

"Isaac . . . you old bastard . . . this was your
doing."

"Yes . . . it was. And I'll tell you something else.
You won't get the marshal's appointment again
either. I'll see to that." Isaac grinned. "You'll have
to retire. You can ride out to my ranch every day.
We'll sit and grow old and play checkers."

"The hell we will!"

The sentence came down from the bench almost
exactly as it had been predicted by both Tom Horn
and Isaac Barr himself. It was all over by eleven
o'clock in the morning. Isaac had added to the list of
names of those invited to his ranch, that of Judge
Riddle. Even before anyone left for the Rocky Barr
ranch however, there was to be another round of
celebrating at Belle Moran's Four Queens saloon.

Isaac Barr had returned to the home of Jim
Bidwell in Nampa. He would return to Boise that
evening for Belle's celebration. Tom Horn was out
of town as well, negotiating the purchase of some
new horses. Lee Morgan had been given quarters in
Belle's place . . . not always alone. On this day, he
was at the livery. Seth Rawlings was more or less
cleaning up the paper work which was now almost
as important as keeping the peace. He'd about
decided to accept the political offer made to him
although he had not yet admitted it aloud.

The door to Seth's office opened and Seth looked

up. Belle Moran stepped in looking scared as hell. She looked back over her shoulder, then she closed the door.

"Belle?" Seth got to his feet.

"Oh Seth . . . Gawd A'mighty . . . I thought it . . . it was over."

"Belle . . . you ain't makin' much sense."

She swallowed, steadied herself on the back of a chair and then moved around in front of it and sat down.

"Three men just walked into my place, Seth, an' took it over. They ran ever'body out an' told me to . . . to fetch the deputy."

"George?"

She shook her head. "Lee. Oh Seth . . . one of 'em is Bryce Kileen . . . Jace's brother. I . . . I don't know the others."

"Jeezus!" Seth thought for a moment. "You see George?"

"No. Seth . . . what . . ." the old marshal held up his hand. He turned, walked to his gun case and pulled out a shotgun.

"Seth!" Belle got to her feet. Seth whirled around. frowning.

"Damn it Belle . . . don't say anythin' . . . you hear me . . . nothin'. I'm still the marshal here an' George Tyson is my deputy . . . not Lee Morgan . . . not anymore. Horn neither. If I can't keep the goddam peace in my own territory, I'd make a piss poor Senator, wouldn't I?"

Belle looked up, tears in her eyes. Still, she knew better than to argue. It was neither the time or the place. Seth loaded the shotgun, put on his heavy coat, pulled on his old, beat up hat and walked around the desk. He leaned down and gently kissed the top of Belle's head. Then, he walked out.

Seth's deputy, George Tyson, had just served some papers on King Gilman over at his feed store. George had mounted up and was headed for the office. Howard Bracken from the Boise newspaper waved him down just half a block away. Bracken had just come from Belle's. He'd gone over to assist with the plans for that night's celebration.

"Mister Bracken," George said smiling, "what can I do for you?" Bracken looked stern.

"Find Lee Morgan. Tom Horn too. Do it fast, George."

"Well Mister Horn's out o' town," George said. "An' last I knew, Mister Morgan was over to the livery barn. What's wrong?"

"Trouble, Deputy. Jace Kileen's brother is down at the Four Queens. He's got two gunmen with him."

"Oh shit!" Tyson yanked his mount's head around, dug his spurs into the animal's flanks and galloped toward the livery. Belle Morgan had regained her composure and was now stricken with the reality of what she had done. She found a pistol . . . an old Navy Colt's. She loaded it, slipped it in the folds of her shawl and hurried off toward her saloon.

Seth Rawlings had just stepped onto Vista Street. He crossed it and started toward the Four Queens. Three blocks away, Tyson galloped up to Lee Morgan who had just emerged from the livery.

"Kileen's brother and two gunmen at Belle's place." Morgan sprang onto Pacer's back.

"Get Seth. Meet me there. Do it, George . . . right now!" Tyson nodded, wheeled his mount and rode off. Morgan spurred Pacer and galloped toward the saloon. He rounded the corner onto Vista with Howard Bracken just behind him. Both saw Seth. The old marshal was just in front of the saloon's doors.

"Seth! Wait!" Seth turned. The bat wings pushed open and a tall, dark haired man stepped out. Seth's head jerked around. The man was carrying a shotgun. He brought it up, stock first, with a sweeping motion from right to left in front of him. The end of the stock caught Seth's jaw and sent the old lawman reeling. He fell from the boardwalk and into the street. He lost his own weapon and lay sprawled, helpless and dazed, at the man's mercy. The man with the shotgun heard the riders to his left, looked up and fired from the hip. The shots struck nothing but forced both Morgan and Bracken to rein up. They dismounted. The man disappeared back inside.

"Morgan," Bracken hollered. "Look!" Morgan did. Toward the other end of the block, Belle Moran came around the corner at sort of a run. She crossed the street and disappeared toward the back of the building.

"Damn," Morgan said. "She'll get herself killed." The tall man stepped out again, the shotgun leveled at Seth.

"Where's Lee Morgan, old man?"

"I'm right here," Morgan shouted. The man glanced up, grinned and turned back to look at Seth. Seth was now trying to sit up and, at the same time, reach his pistol. The man brought the shotgun to his shoulder. Morgan drew. A shot ran out from the opposite end of the street. A rifle! The man's grin faded. He staggered. The shotgun discharged harmlessly into the air. The man fell back through the bat wing doors. Morgan, Bracken and Seth all turned toward the sound of the rifle. George Tyson was walking toward them.

Morgan, in a crouch and moving fast, emptied the

Smith and Wesson into the big, plate glass window just to the left of the door at the Four Queens. He could only hope to God, he'd hit no one unless it was one of the two remaining gunmen. In any event, Tyson and Bracken got Seth, who was growling at them as usual, to his feet and out of the way. His jaw was broken.

Morgan pressed against the building, reloaded the pistol and Tyson scooped up Seth's shotgun and tossed it to Morgan. Morgan holstered the pistol. Bracken moved down the block, helping Seth. Tyson squeezed into a doorway across the street.

Inside the saloon, Belle Moran started down the stairs. She was wearing a low cut, emerald green, satin dress. Her left hand was tugging at the bodice, pulling it lower, revealing more of her creamy, ample bosom. Her right hand, behind the folds of the dress, concealed the old Colt's.

"You gents want a drink—it's on the house?"

The tall man who had been shot was not dead. A second man, stocky of build and dirty looking, was crouched down examining the tall man's wound. He stood up, turned, drew a pistol and pointed it at Belle.

"Reese," a man at the bar yelled, "is that any way to treat a lady? Particularly our hostess."

"She's the one brought the goddam law in, Bryce."

"Take care of Shell," Bryce Kileen said, smiling. "I'll take care of the lady."

Belle moved behind the bar, stopped and smiled. She let out the breath of air she'd been holding when she saw the man named Reese holster his pistol.

"What'll you have?" Belle asked, realizing the shakiness in her own voice. Bryce Kileen, a sinister smile on his face, leaned foward, grabbed a handful of Belle's hair, jerked forward, hard and twisted.

"I'll have that pistol you're hiding . . . you goddam whore!" Belle had brought her arm up reflexively, and Kileen now grabbed it and twisted. Belle let out a cry of pain. Kileen took the gun and then shoved Belle backwards. "You get over to the front door and you tell Lee Morgan to come inside if you want to stay alive."

Belle nodded. She couldn't help but wonder how Bryce Kileen had known about the pistol. A moment later, she got her answer. As she walked past the stairway, she caught a faint movement above her on the balcony. She looked up. Kileen had two more men up there!

Reese walked to the bar. "Shell took one through the side. Got the bleedin' stopped. Bullet went clean through. Think he's got a busted rib. He'll need a doc."

"We'll get one," Bryce said.

Belle shouted. "Lee . . . they . . . they want you inside." There was no answer. "Lee . . . it's Belle . . . they . . ." She stopped. Tyson was in a doorway exactly opposite her, across the street. He was motioning to her to come through the door.

Belle took a deep breath, pushed hard on both bat wing doors and hurried through. Instantly, Lee Morgan had her by the arm, jerked her aside and pushed her down. Two shots smashed into the doors where, a moment before, Belle had been standing. Morgan, in a crouch, wheeled himself in front of the door and fired . . . up . . . toward the top of the stairs. He heard a grunt, the clatter of a gun against wood and a body bouncing down the stairway. Morgan threw himself in the opposite direction and came back to his feet . . . his back pressed against the wall on the opposite side of the door.

"Belle . . . stay close to the buildings until you get to the corner . . . then go like hell . . . get to the depot. Stay put!"

Belle didn't argue. She paused when she reached the alley way which led to the back of the saloon. She turned back to wave at Morgan. Instead, she saw George Tyson. His eyes were big and round. He raised his rifle and fired. The shot was so close, Belle could hear the bullet splitting the air ahead of it. The other man who'd been on the balcony had slipped out the back, worked his way along the alley and was waiting to kill her as soon as she stepped into view. Tyson killed him but not without sacrifice.

George had to show himself in order to make the shot. Across the street in the Four Queens, Reese had just moved to the broken window and peered out. Tyson was a full, close target. Reese drew and fired. Tyson went down, critically wounded. Reese dived for cover. Morgan put three rounds through the window. None hit home.

"Kileen . . . you bastard . . . walk out. . . you and me . . . same as with Jace." Morgan waited. No reply. "You got one man shot up, two dead. Let's settle it."

"Fuck you, Morgan." Morgan turned. Belle was still at the corner. She was crying. She was looking at Tyson writhing in pain across the street.

"Belle," Morgan shouted, "go on . . . now . . . do what I told you to do." She finally moved . . . slowly . . . in a daze.

"Morgan!"

"Yeah, Kileen . . . I'm still here."

"You got a marshal with a busted jaw an' a dyin' deputy out there. You ain't a goddam bit better off than me. Why don't *you* come in?" Kileen laughed.

"Fuck you," Morgan said. Inside the saloon, Reese had worked his way back to the bar. Bryce Kileen was now at its far end where cover was but a few feet away.

"Get on up stairs. We got nobody coverin' the back." Reese nodded. Kileen took a bottle, moved to a corner table, upended the table next to it so that he would have some handy cover, sat down, uncorked the jug and took a long pull. "Let 'im know we're in here," Kileen hollered at Reese. Reese was about half way up the stairs. He turned, drew and fanned four shots into the bat wing doors. He grinned, holstered the pistol and turned back.

"Oh Jeezus," Reese shouted. His eyes were big, his mouth still open, his gut tightened into a ball of fear. His eyes were level with both barrels of a Parker shotgun. He might have seen the powder flash as they discharged . . . then Reese's head disappeared.

"Just Kileen now," Tom Horn said, "all by himself, Morgan."

"I'll be goddamned," Morgan whispered to himself, grinning. "That ol' son-of-a-bitch always manages to be in the right place at the right time." Morgan loaded the Smith and Wesson, holstered it, turned, pushed through the splintered bat wings and moved into the center of the saloon. Bryce Kileen was on his feet. He set the empty jug back on the table. Shell tried to draw. Morgan killed him.

"Seems like your hand," Bryce said, grinning.

"Make your move, Kileen."

"Oh no . . . no, Mister Morgan. I don't think so. Man with the shotgun up there . . . whole goddam town ready to string me up . . . even if I killed you, I got no way out. No sir, Mister Morgan. You'll have to take me in an' do it the hard way. I'll be around.

Mebbe I'll break out. Mebbe I got more men waitin' outside o' town. Hell, I ain't shot nobody in Boise,'' he laughed, ''mebbe they'll find me innocent an' I'll jist ride away. Anyway . . . you'll never have to stick around to find out . . . or keep lookin' over your shoulder.''

Morgan looked toward the balcony. Tom Horn stood there, cradling the Parker. Their eyes met. Tom had seen the expression before . . . many times . . . mostly on his own face. Now, seeing it on someone else's . . . it bothered him. He frowned and, almost imperceptibly, gave a negative shake of his head. It was too late.

Lee Morgan drew the little, short barreled Smith and Wesson he'd gotten from drummer Mason. He'd probably never made a faster or smoother draw . . . even though no one was drawing against him. He was just as accurate as he was fast. Kileen died instantly, a bullet between his eyes.

Epilogue

Tom Horn lied about the last few minutes at the Four Queens saloon in Boise, Idaho. He told Seth Parker there had been a shoot-out. Tom then rode out . . . Wyoming bound . . . riding to his own destiny. Seth would have believed the lie . . . save for one thing. Lee Morgan left a letter which told the truth. He hadn't been wearing the badge that day. He'd quit the law. He gunned down Bryce Kileen in cold blood. Then, he rode out.

Seth Rawlings was faced with one, final, painful duty as a U.S. marshal. He knew Morgan would understand. Seth had to do it. Once again, sheriffs' offices would all possess a wanted poster on Lee Morgan. *Wanted: For the Murder of Bryce Kileen in Boise, Idaho.* Seth did his duty, resigned and became one of the state's most respected senators. George Tyson survived his wounds and lived out his life as a United States marshal.

Belle Moran sold the Four Queens about a year later, moved to San Francisco, flourished for a few more years and then disappeared into obscurity.

Judge Isaac Barr died, quietly, at the Rocky Barr ranch about eighteen months after Idaho's darkest period ended. The coroner said his death was from heart failure. Many believed his heart was simply broken and never mended again.

The initial manhunt for Lee Morgan was ambitious and extensive. Morgan anticipated his pursuers. Well supplied, he stayed hidden until the search for him had become more passive than active. Summer had returned to the Idaho wilderness before he stirred again. He rode Pacer slowly to the summit of a spiny ridge on a fine, sunny morning in July. He stopped, stood up in the stirrups, turned and took his final look into the rocky fortress at the base of the Bitterroots. Then, he rode away from Gunsmoke Gorge.